BROKEN INNOCENCE

A BROKEN REBEL BROTHERHOOD NOVEL

ANDI RHODES

Copyright © 2020 by Andi Rhodes

All rights reserved.

No part of this book may be reproduced in any form or by any electronic or mechanical means, including information storage and retrieval systems, without written permission from the author, except for the use of brief quotations in a book review.

Cover Artwork – © 2020 L.J. Anderson of Mayhem Cover Creations

For my mom, who has never wavered in her support and belief in me, who is always just a phone call away no matter what, who has listened to me go on and on for HOURS about nothing and everything, and who has been one of my greatest cheerleaders throughout this incredible journey. I love you mom!

ALSO BY ANDI RHODES

Broken Rebel Brotherhood

Broken Souls

Broken Innocence

Broken Boundaries

Broken Rebel Brotherhood: Complete Series Box set

Broken Rebel Brotherhood: Next Generation

Broken Hearts

Broken Wings

Broken Mind

Bastards and Badges

Stark Revenge

Slade's Fall

Jett's Guard

Soulless Kings MC

Fender

Joker

Piston

Greaser

Riker

Trainwreck

Squirrel

Gibson

Satan's Legacy MC

Snow's Angel

Toga's Demons

Magic's Torment

"Life had broken her;
just as it had broken him.
But when they got together,
their pieces became whole.
And they continued on
their journey, together,
mended as one."

~Steve Maraboli

PROLOGUE

BRIE

Thump thump… thump thump… thump thump…

My heartbeat echoed in my ears as consciousness seeped in. Humid air permeated my lungs, carrying traces of dirt with it. Confusion clouded my brain when I registered a musty smell. Something wasn't right. I was supposed to be at a barbecue, surrounded by my friends, not curled up on a dirt floor with a throbbing headache.

Dry soil sifted through my fingers as I leveraged myself up on shaky arms, wincing as tiny pebbles dug into my palms. My body felt as if something were weighing me down, but there was nothing. There was a shred of light that was swallowed up by surrounding darkness, and I had to blink several times before my eyes adjusted to the single flickering bulb swinging above me on a string.

My last memory flickered through my mind like a movie reel, and I felt as if I'd been sucker-punched.

Sadie's face draining of color… The butt of the gun crashing against my temple…

Zach had done this.

I realized the error in my thinking and shook my head to clear the cobwebs. Not Zach... Ian.

"Where the fuck am I?" My voice echoed in the cavernous space around me.

As a Veteran, I had the training to size up any situation, both quickly and accurately, but I wasn't firing on all cylinders. My thoughts were groggy and my movements sluggish, as if some sort of drug was coursing through my system.

"I thought you'd never wake up." A deep voice sounded from the shadows and adrenaline surged through my veins. I whipped around toward the sound and pain shot through me from my toes on up, causing me to immediately regret the movement.

Don't let them see your fear. The voice in my head was a mantra from my military days.

"Who the hell are you?" I demanded of the unfamiliar figure now standing before me. I let my gaze travel up and down his gangly body, trying to determine if I'd ever seen him before.

Nope.

Green eyes stared back at me, but I couldn't tell if they were really *seeing* me. They looked a bit maniacal. *I'd remember those eyes.*

"I wasn't sure how much Etorphine to inject. I'm glad to see it didn't kill you." The way he smiled as he said that scared me more than I cared to admit. I'd seen smiles like that before. It was the smile of someone who thought causing pain was like a Sunday stroll through the park.

"I'm Steve, by the way," he said as he extended his hand to shake mine. *Yeah, right!*

"Steve?" That seemed like such a normal name. A *nice* name.

No reply. *Okay, moving on.* I scratched my head as a million questions flooded my mind.

"Etorphine?" It was the first question I could put voice to. Of course, I had more, but I was too afraid of the answers, so I held them in. For now.

"Well, pretty," I cringed at the term, "Ian would have a fit if I killed you, but he doesn't mind if I play a little." Steve laughed and it sounded like pure evil.

"But… how… why…?" I stammered, hating myself for the small display of emotion.

"Because." He started pacing back and forth. He appeared agitated now, so I let him work out whatever problem was going on in that crazy mind of his. "Ian called and told me he had a problem." The pacing stopped and Steve stood only a foot away, coldly staring at my tits. "A pretty problem."

My fist shot out, connecting with his jaw. His neck snapped back, reminding me of a bobble-head, and the sound of bone breaking fueled my rage. I continued to pummel his face and reveled in the blood that sprayed from his nose. Steve tried to block my attack by throwing up his arms, but he couldn't keep up with my adrenaline induced energy.

As much fun as it was to take my anger and fear out on him, my knuckles were bruised and bleeding and my body started to slow down. I had no fight left in me.

"Fuck you, asshole." I spat at Steve's prone body, now lying in the dirt.

Dizziness washed over me, and I swayed. I'd pushed myself too far. My ass hit the ground, and I fell to my back, holding my head in my hands. I needed to get my wits about me if I wanted to get out of this hell. Steve groaned and I managed to lift my head and ascertain that he was still lying there, bloody. The fact that he was able to manage any sound at all told me just how little time I had to escape. Men like him fell, but rarely did they stay down as long as you hoped.

I rolled to my stomach and forced myself up to my knees,

ignoring the tilt-a-whirl feeling. After assuring myself I wasn't going to end up on my ass again, I stood, resting my hands on my thighs. My lungs burned from the exertion of the fight and it took me several more minutes before I felt confident in my ability to actually put one foot in front of the other.

The door was across the room, if one could call it that, and when I reached it, I twisted the knob. I didn't really think it would open, but I had to try. I pounded against the barrier and yelled out, praying that someone, anyone, would hear me. My arms tired quickly, still overworked from beating Steve, and I let them fall to my sides. Defeat wasn't an option, but I had to face the fact that the easy way out wasn't going to be *my* way out.

"Okay, what would *he* do?" Talking out loud, I ran through our Survival, Evasion, Resistance, and Escape training. It had saved my ass before and it would now. "First, I need to—"

Pain shot through my skull as I was dragged away from the door by my hair. I reached back to grab the source of my agony and ease the burn in my scalp but came up empty. I dug my heels in, trying to stop from being dragged farther from freedom and only managed to slow it down a little.

"Motherfucker!" If physical action wouldn't work, maybe name-calling would.

Get real, Brie. You're only going to antagonize him.

Steve was now standing with his legs braced apart on either side of my hips. He stared down at me, blood trickling from his nose.

"Don't ever do that again!" Steve screamed, sounding more commanding than I gave him credit for. He wiped the crimson from his face with the back of his hand, only managing to smear it across his cheeks to his hairline.

"Do what?" I countered, trying to sit up.

Shut up, Brie!

His face contorted with rage just before his boot connected with my chest and I flew back, hitting my head on the dirt floor. Stars sparkled behind my eyelids, and I fought to maintain consciousness. Even though passing out was not an option, I kept my eyes closed, in hopes that he'd back off, even if for a minute or two.

When he didn't kick me again, I took a chance and opened my eyes to slits. Steve was pacing back and forth, muttering incoherently. When he turned back to look at me, I squeezed my eyes shut.

"Why did you make me do that?" He was close. Too close. But he didn't sound as crazed as he had a few minutes before.

I ignored his question and peered up at him. We stared at each other, both silent, but both speaking volumes with our glares.

He started pacing again, and I tracked his every movement. The longer he paced, the calmer he appeared.

"I had to bring you here. Ian will understand. He'll see. I'm doing this for him." Steve wasn't talking to me, but rather to whoever, or whatever, was in his head with him.

"Doing what for him?"

I wasn't entirely sure I wanted the answer.

I watched as he went to the door and bent over to pick something up. I tracked his every move as he pulled a Ziploc bag out of a camouflage backpack and threw it at me. I glanced down as it sent dust clouds billowing, and I struggled to stop the coughing fit it elicited. Once I had my hacking under control, I squinted to see what was in the bag and had to school my expression. *Food.* At least I'd be able to eat. Build up my strength. I'd bide my time, strategize, plan. I was good at that. And then I'd get the fuck out.

"Eat up."

"I'm not hungry," I lied. My stomach chose that moment to growl, filling the space with its intensity.

"Fine," he snickered. *Bastard.*

As I watched him leave, I listened for the telltale signs of a lock. The sharp clank of metal echoed in the space, and I let myself relax a little, sighing as some of the tension left my body. I picked up the bag he had tossed, opened it and sniffed its contents. Beef Jerky. As I pulled a piece out and brought it to my lips, a shiver raced through me and my thoughts spiraled out of control.

How long had I been gone? Has the BRB noticed I'm missing? Will they find me? Are they even looking for me?

"Of course they are." I ate the rest of the meager offering and berated myself for such thoughts.

If anyone could find me, it was *him*.

1

GRIFFIN

Seven months later...

𝓘 couldn't find her. I'd looked. Goddamn, had I looked. But it was like she was a ghost. As if the worst day of my life had never happened. She wasn't and it had. I knew that. My brothers knew that. Jackson knew that.

Enough! This was not the time for this.

Standing in the living room of the Broken Rebel Brotherhood's main house, I listened with half an ear to the sound of the car pulling up in the driveway. Micah Mallory, our president, and my best friend, was bringing home his twins today. Twins. Fuck, I couldn't believe it.

"They're here!" Nell's voice filtered into my thoughts and I forced myself to smile at her.

"Come on, Griffin," Nell whined as she tugged on my sleeve. "Don't be such an asshole. Not today."

"I'm not an asshole, Half-pint." The nickname I'd given her shortly after being assigned to the same Navy Seal team earned me a punch to the gut. I grunted at the impact. Nell was a lot stronger than she looked.

"Oh, suck it up," she teased, releasing my shirt. "We both know I didn't hurt you." She stuck her tongue out at me like a child, reminding me of what I loved about her. Nell was like a sister to me and had helped me through some very dark days the last few months. Hell, the last few years really.

"Okay, Half-pint, let's go see those babies." I slung my arm around her shoulder and pulled her to me. She settled into my side, and for a moment, we both stood there, unmoving. I didn't know if we were both thinking the same thing, but the silence that settled over the room made me think we did.

She should be here.

Neither of us spoke as we made our way to the door. My cell phone buzzed against my thigh, but I ignored it. When we stepped out onto the big wraparound front porch, Aiden was sitting in one of the rocking chairs, his dog at his feet. Doc was standing on the steps, ready to lend a hand to the new parents, should they need it. I looked out toward the driveway and watched as Micah helped Sadie out of the backseat. He wound his fingers through her hair and kissed her.

The jealousy that snaked through me was surprising and extremely unwanted. We'd served in the military together, and after our last mission, we'd been broken. All of us for different reasons. We went our separate ways for a while, to lick our wounds, I suppose. Micah was the one that brought us all back together. Nell, Aiden, Brie and myself. Doc joined the Brotherhood a bit later, but he had served as well.

If ever there was someone who deserved happiness, it was Micah and his fiancé, Sadie. They were perfect together, and I was happy for them. But *she* should be here.

I stepped away from Nell and jogged down the steps toward the pair at the car. As much as I wanted to run the other way, away from the emotions, I knew I couldn't. Not today.

"Break it up, you two," I called as I neared them. I pulled Sadie out of Micah's arms and wrapped her up in a big hug, lifting her off the ground.

"Hey, mama," I said against her cheek.

"Hey, Griff." Sadie laughed.

It still amazed me that she could laugh. She'd been beaten to within an inch of her life on multiple occasions and she still found the strength to live and love and trust. She was strong as hell, and I admired her for it.

"Hands off my woman." A shadow loomed as Micah's large form appeared behind me. There was no heat in his tone, but I released her all the same.

"Oh, Griffin, wait until you see them." Sadie beamed as she turned to get one bundle out of the car.

"I have seen them. They can't have changed much since yesterday," I said, which earned me a smirk thrown over her shoulder.

"Brother, you have no idea." Micah reached in after Sadie and got the second bundle. Blue and pink. One for each of them. Just then the pink bundle, Isabelle, let out a shriek and Isaiah soon followed.

"Babies are hungry, sweetness," Micah announced and then turned toward me.

"Griffin, can you grab the rest of the stuff out of the trunk while I help Sadie get these two inside?"

"Sure thing," I said as I rounded the vehicle. In a moment of weakness, my gaze followed the new family as they made their way up the steps and through the front door. Aiden's eyes caught mine and my head snapped down.

As I was grabbing the bags out of the trunk, footsteps crunched on the gravel behind me. Out of the corner of my eye, I saw Aiden and Doc stop next to the car and fold their arms across their chests. They could intimidate almost anyone, but not me.

"What?" I demanded, glaring at them. "Are you going to just stand there or are you going to help me?"

"You seem to have it under control," Doc quipped.

I held my middle fingers in the air. One for each of them. "Fuck you."

"No thanks," Aiden said. "You're not really my type."

"Shut it." Venom laced my words. I flung a bag at his chest, letting all of my frustration show. My muscles stiffened when he caught it with ease.

"That's it. Take it out on all of us who— "

"Are you assholes coming or not?"

Saved by the Nell. I reminded myself to thank her later for ending that before it could get too ugly. I knew where it had been headed and I wasn't ready for that.

After getting everything out of the car, I slammed the trunk and shoved my way past my brothers. Both grunted, but neither said another word as we carried everything inside, depositing it by the door.

I hesitated in the entryway as memories assailed me. Memories of *that* night. Reaching for the gun in my waistband, sweeping the house for any sign of life. The blood. *Her* blood.

The blind fury and fear were as real to me in that moment as they were seven months ago. I started to reach for that same gun before a piercing cry broke through my thoughts and I remembered that those moments were over. Shoving my now shaking hands through my hair, I forced myself to take a few deep breaths and calm down. There were babies in the house for fucks sake.

"You all right, man?" Micah asked, his tone serious.

"Yeah. Yeah, I'm fine. It's just…" He wouldn't understand. Nobody would.

"I know, Griff." Micah placed his hand on my shoulder. I didn't bother trying to remove it. Micah wouldn't budge. "We'll find her. You've gotta believe that."

"Alive or dead?" I whispered.

"Huh?"

"Yes, we'll find her," I lifted my eyes to the ceiling and blew out a frustrated breath. "But will it be alive or dead?"

"She's a fighter, Griffin. We're going to bring her home." Micah's head twisted toward the kitchen as another cry rang out. He turned back to me and squeezed my shoulder. "We won't stop until we do." And then he was gone.

Of course we'd bring her home. I knew that. *Leave no man behind.* Dead or alive. Jesus, let her be alive.

I followed the sounds of laughter and made my way into the kitchen, pausing at the door and taking in the sight of my family. No one acknowledged my presence, and that suited me fine. Nell was putting some snacks out for everyone. Micah and Sadie each held a baby, swaying to calm them. Doc and Aiden sat at the bar shoveling food into their mouths as quickly as it hit the counter.

She should be here.

I rubbed the ache in my chest as I walked the rest of the way into the space.

"Finally." Nell winked to soften the comment.

"Sorry," I mumbled to no one in particular. No one acknowledged the apology, nor had I expected them to. I knew they weren't angry with me for my broodiness, and certainly, they had an idea of the cause. With our shared past, most of us had PTSD, causing some *off* days. Sure, I'd been cranky and anti-social more than usual, but they understood why. Partially, anyway.

The next hour was as close to fun as it could get. We ate, joked, laughed, and ribbed each other. We talked about our time together in the Navy Seals, regaling Sadie with more stories than she probably wanted to hear. It all felt so... normal.

She should be here.

As Doc was reminiscing about his first day with the BRB, my phone vibrated in my pocket. I ignored it, wanting to stay present in the moment. When it vibrated again, and again, I gave in and took it out of my jeans. After swiping my finger over the screen, I punched in the passcode, and my stomach dropped as I read text messages from Jackson, the Sheriff.

Jackson: Possible break in the case.

Jackson: We need you. Be at my office in half an hour.

Jackson: Where are you?

Jackson: Call me, dammit!

Damn, that'd been over an hour ago. When I read the last one, my stomach completely bottomed out.

Jackson: We found her!

2

BRIE

"Look at me!"

Rough fingers dug into my cheeks and forced my gaze to Steve's face. I hated the malicious lust I saw there. Even more than that, I hated what I knew was reflected in my eyes. *Nothing.*

As I lay there in the dirt staring at pure evil, I tried to block out the sound of slapping flesh as he worked to find release. Shame washed over me in waves, matching the intensity of his thrusts. Layer upon layer of humiliation piled on top of me until I couldn't breathe. Couldn't see. Couldn't *feel.*

That was his ultimate goal. It was ironic, really. The one thing that I'd used to chase away my demons was being used against me.

On day two, I'd woken up alone and in desperate need of a bathroom. My eyes darted around the dark cave, seeking out my options, when they landed on a bucket. A mixture of relief and disgust coursed through me, and that was when the first crack in my armor occurred.

There was nothing left of it now.

After taking care of my most basic need, I'd taken the time to really examine my surroundings. A combination of rock and dirt surrounded me on all four sides, interrupted only by a wooden door. I wish I'd known then what I know now. There was no way out. That door was reinforced by a steel insert, and no amount of kicking and banging could open it. Not only had that resulted in numerous bruises and what I suspected was a broken foot, but when I was caught, Steve beat me bloody.

For the first two weeks, I'd fought like hell. Every chance I got, I let my military training take over. I'd managed to get the drop on him several times and get to the door, but I'd never been able to get through it. It hadn't taken Steve long to figure out that I wasn't going to make things easy on him, so he started to look for a weakness. He hadn't had to search long. The first time he came at me with a syringe of Etorphine, I hadn't been able to hide my fear. I despised needles and just the sight of them had me curled in a ball in an almost catatonic state. I eventually quit fighting. If I didn't fight, no needle.

Surprisingly enough, he hadn't been violent since that second day. The only time he ever raised his hand to me in that two week span was when I tried to fight or when he drugged me. That all changed the day he found out Ian wasn't being released from jail.

After that, I'd learned quickly that not only was Steve crazy, he was vicious. His mood swings came and went so fast that trying to keep up with them caused me mental whiplash. I stopped trying.

Steve had a routine that he rarely wavered from. He never let me out of whatever hole I was being hidden in, but he did visit every day. Sometimes he would be there for minutes and other times, it was hours. Always at dinnertime. He cleaned out my bucket each day and had the decency to keep me stocked with basic supplies. Toilet paper, toothbrush, toothpaste, soap and bottled water. Apparently, he drew the line at fucking a dirty vag. I'd ignored the soap, hoping he would be turned off. I'd been so wrong. Three days of not washing resulted in a beating that had left a piercing pain in my chest and headaches that made me think I had a concussion. He hadn't granted me a reprieve on the fucking either. Clean or dirty didn't matter to him.

"Fuck me!" Steve shouted out his release.

I rolled to my side as soon as he pulled out and curled into a ball, wishing he would return my clothes to me, but knowing he wouldn't. I hadn't been allowed to have my clothes since he'd found out about Ian. It was like that information was the key to unlocking his true self, and he no longer had to be careful.

Steve slapped my ass as he stood up and began dressing.

"That was fun. Maybe next time you could at least pretend you're enjoying it," he said as he pulled his shirt over his head and prepared to leave.

"Never," I whispered.

"What was that?"

He leaned over me, hot breath coasting over my cheek.

"Nothing."

"That's what I thought." As he stood back up, my eyes tracked his movement, caught between not giving a shit what he did and needing to know if he was indeed done for the day.

"You're dinner's over there." He pointed toward the corner where there was now a table and chair for me to sit and eat. "Be a good girl and eat up. I'd hate to have to punish you for wasting food."

With that pronouncement, he walked out the door, and I stared at the closed barrier. After several seconds, I looked around me and my gaze landed on the scratches on the wall.

Tally marks. Two hundred and twelve of them. One for each day I'd been here. I'd started out using my fingernails but those quickly disappeared, and my fingertips had become raw. The dirt floor was littered with the stones I'd used next, but those were so tiny I couldn't use any more than once. Most of the stones lay in a pile underneath and were stained with blood.

After two months of captivity, Steve had broken me. In the military, we'd been taught survival and I'd always thought I could withstand anything. I was wrong. So very wrong. No amount of training could have prepared me for what I'd faced at the hands of this beast.

Hope no longer flared that I'd be rescued. Hell, I quit believing that anyone was even looking for me. So certain that *he* would find me, I'd died a little when I had to face reality.

He wasn't coming.

All those tally marks and I was still here. Trapped in a very real horror movie where the monster wouldn't be defeated.

My gaze moved from the wall to the table where my food was. Despite the grumbling of my stomach, I cringed at the sight of it. Turkey sandwich—sans mayonnaise—and a bag of chips. The turkey sandwich was the constant. Every once in a while he'd switch up the kind of chips he gave me, sour cream and onion this time. I hated sour cream and onion. Every day the food would mock me from the plate while I debated whether or not to eat it. There were days where I wouldn't eat and prayed for death, but my hunger always won out. Today, my hunger wouldn't win.

I stood and stalked to the plate before picking it up. The sound of glass shattering as I threw it at the door echoed in the space. Broken shards joined the hundreds of others on the ground from the numerous plates I'd thrown before. I walked over and bent to pick up the largest piece I could find. After retrieving it, I returned to my spot along the wall. Glass embedded in the soles of my feet and left a trail of blood in the dirt as I walked. I didn't care.

As I slid down to the floor, I pressed the shard to my wrist. My wide eyes stared at it for several moments, anger surfacing as if it was taunting me. *Do it. Just do it already.* The voices in my head repeated that command. Over and over until a wet trickle ran down my arm.

The voices stopped, probably thinking they'd won, and reason returned. I tossed the glass as far away from me as I could and glared at the crimson line on my forearm.

My mind made up to live another day, I curled back into a ball and prayed for sleep. At least in sleep, there was a chance I would be somewhere else. Anywhere else. Even if it was only in my dreams, it was a welcome reprieve from my waking nightmare. Who knew? Maybe I'd even get to see *him*.

A lone tear snaked from my dirt-caked eyelids and down my cheek. Sleep took me sometime later.

"You're so beautiful, Brie," he said as he swept a loose strand of hair off my cheek.

"Thanks," I mumbled, shy all of a sudden. I was never good at receiving compliments and always felt awkward when it happened.

"You don't need to thank me for speaking the truth. I could look at you for hours, and it would still not be enough." He breathed in my ear and a sweet ache bloomed between my thighs.

I shivered as he nipped at my earlobe and traced his tongue in a fiery path from there to my lips. My hips gyrated into his, craving contact. His mouth never left mine as his hands skimmed my flesh, causing goosebumps to spread over me. I ran my fingers through his chestnut brown hair and tugged when his hands reached the globes of my ass and squeezed.

"Brie," he breathed between kisses.

"Brie!" he yelled.

Wait, why was he yelling?

"Brie! Oh God, Brie!" The yelling continued.

As bright light seeped through my closed lids, my body coiled in on itself. I didn't want to leave my dream. It was the only peace I'd been able to find over the last seven months.

"Brie, you need to wake up, baby. Come on, open your eyes."

Baby? Why did the voice sound so familiar?

Recognition flared and my eyes jerked open. I jackknifed into a sitting position and threw my arm up to block the blinding light. I'd been in darkness for so long that the white light was unbearable.

"Turn that off!"

The demand was immediately followed by a dimming of the light. As my eyes adjusted to the change, I found myself staring into familiar eyes. Eyes of a man I thought had forgotten me.

Was he real?

Not wanting the answer, I squeezed my eyes shut.

"Come on, baby. Don't do that." He ran his fingers down my cheek and cupped my chin. "You're safe now. We're going to take you home."

My mouth opened and closed several times before any words came out.

"Y-you came." My voice was unrecognizable, even to my ears. Speech had often resulted in retribution, so I hadn't talked much.

"Ambulance is five minutes out." Another voice invaded the moment and awareness seeped in. We weren't alone.

"Good. Toss me a blanket."

I listened to this short exchange with indifference. He was trying to help me maintain some dignity by covering me up, but I'd long ago quit caring about my nudity. Modesty was a thing of the past. Soft fabric covered me, but I made no move to hold it in place.

"Can you stand? Walk?" The questions registered, but I couldn't answer. The ground had suddenly become the most interesting thing in the world.

"No? Okay. I'm going to pick you up and carry you, baby." Strong arms came around my back and under my knees, and I was suddenly above the ground. Not looking at the face of my rescuer, I buried my head in his neck. The second my skin made contact with his, I lost control.

Sobs wracked my body as he carried me out of my prison and into the fresh air. I flung my arms around him and held on tight as the sound of sirens seemed to harmonize with my cries. Not letting go when he tried to transfer me from his arms to a gurney, I had one thought that played on repeat.

He came. Griffin came.

3

GRIFFIN

*P*ain shot through my knuckles as my fist connected with the wall. I hated waiting and that's exactly what I'd been doing for the last few hours. Brie was in with the doctor, and no one would tell me a damn thing.

As I paced, my mind played back the afternoon leading up to Brie's rescue. After receiving the text from Jackson that he thought he'd found her, I'd shown the others and then raced out of the house, not bothering to see if anyone followed. When I arrived at the police station, Jackson already had a team waiting and ready to go.

"Where is she?" I demanded, my face an inch from Jackson's. I knew I was crossing some invisible line and didn't give a damn.

"We think she's being held by the old Indian Mounds."

"Being held? You mean, she's alive?" I held my breath as I waited for the answer to a question I was sure would devastate me.

"We think so. We've had every department in the state assisting with this investigation. That eventually paid off." Jackson took a deep breath and stared at me for a long minute.

"Spit it out, Jackson. What the fuck aren't you telling me?"

"We think Ian had a partner." He bowed his head as he spoke. *He undoubtedly knew this new information would set off a whole new rage in me.*

"No fucking way! You told me you were monitoring his calls. You told me that they hadn't led to anything." I shook my head, not understanding this recent bit of information.

"That was true, until yesterday. Ian's trial is coming up, and maybe he got desperate. I don't know. But he placed a call and it all felt off, *so I followed up on it."* A smile slowly bloomed on Jackson's face. *"He slipped up, Griffin. We tracked down the guy he called and put a tail on him. He left his farm this afternoon and traveled to a location where we think Brie could be."*

"But you don't know?" Tension rippled through my shoulders.

"The officer tailing him reported back that the suspect went into what appeared to be a door in the Indian Mound and was inside for about a half-hour before he came out, emptied a bucket and went back in. As of ten minutes ago, he was still inside."

"Why the fuck hasn't your guy gone in?"

"Because, we don't know what we're dealing with. We don't know if Brie's there. If he leaves, my guy has been instructed to follow but not engage. We'll send back-up to make an arrest if it comes to that." Jackson seemed pretty pleased with himself, but I wasn't yet convinced. *"Griffin, man, Ian slipped up. We're finally going to get to bring Brie home."*

"But nobody's actually had eyes on Brie?" Fury took hold at the lack of confirmation that Brie was indeed at the location, and I got in Jackson's face.

"Griffin, you need to back off before I regret pulling you in on this. The only reason you're here is because I know a friendly face will go a long way with Brie if she's there. Who knows what she's been through the last seven months? I don't want to traumatize her more than she already is."

"Well, then, let's go!" Not waiting for any instructions, I stalked to my bike and climbed on.

The moment I laid eyes on her in that prison, I'd been gutted. Shock had coursed through me at the sight of her naked body, covered in dirt, bruises, and blood. The look in her eyes when she'd seen me had done nothing to calm me down. It had been similar to that of a feral cat. *How had she survived?*

Her captor had been gone by the time we got there, and he'd also managed to evade his tail. Apparently, the officer had been forced to stop at a railroad crossing. *Goddamn train.* I'd given Jackson's people hell for their incompetence until he'd threatened to throw me in jail. Brie would need me, so I'd shut my mouth.

"Any news?" Doc asked.

My head snapped in his direction, and my pacing ceased. When had he gotten there?

"Nothing yet." I shook my head. "Where's Emersyn? Can't she find out something for us? Maybe get me in to see her?" Doc's girlfriend was a nurse at this hospital, and I was hoping she could pull a few strings.

"She's not on shift tonight, but I texted her. She should be here any minute."

Just then, Emersyn walked through the automatic double doors, as if Doc had conjured her with his words.

"Hi Maddoc." Normally I'd give Doc shit about his given name, but not now. As Doc pulled her in for a hug, I found myself torn between demanding that they hurry up their little greeting and jealousy because I wanted what they had. "How is she?"

"Aw, Jesus, Em. It's bad." Doc looked to me to continue.

"These assholes won't tell us anything. But, yeah, it's bad." My emotions didn't filter into my words, but they were there. Just under the surface, waiting to break free. "She was being held in a cave. I don't know much. Yet. She's being assessed by the ER doc now, but I suspect she'll be admitted.

There's no way she'll be released tonight. Not in the condition she was in."

"I'm so sorry, guys. I never thought... Brie... wow, I just can't believe it. She's alive." Emersyn laid her hand on my arm as she spoke, but I didn't feel the comfort I imagined she was trying to give. As she pulled her hand away, she squared her shoulders. "Give me a few minutes to see what I can find out." With that, she walked toward the ER bay—where Brie was being examined—and disappeared behind the flimsy blue curtain.

I resumed pacing as I waited for news. Doc left to find Aiden and Nell. They'd gone to get coffee earlier and had yet to return. The rustling of the curtain caught my attention. My head snapped up and my eyes bore a hole into Emersyn. The defeated look in her eyes caused my heart rate to spike, and I braced myself for what she would tell me.

"How is she? Can I see her? Did she tell you anything?" My questions spilled from me in rapid succession.

"You can't see her yet." My eyes narrowed but she ignored it and pressed on. "Griffin, she's got a long road ahead of her." Emersyn's eyes shifted to the others as they walked up behind me.

"Hold up. Let me call Micah. He'll want an update." Aiden speed-dialed Micah and we all silently waited for him to answer.

"'Hey,'" Micah's voice sounded through the speaker. I didn't hear Sadie or the babies in the background, telling me Micah was in the library, no doubt to protect Sadie from any details.

"Hey, Mic. Emersyn was just about to fill us in. Thought you'd want to hear," Aiden said.

"Damn straight."

All eyes turned to Emersyn in silent invitation for her to continue.

"As I was telling Griffin, Brie's recovery isn't going to be an easy one. From what I could tell, she's lost quite a bit of weight. She's malnourished and weak. The doctors are still assessing her physical injuries and she'll be admitted until further notice." Emersyn glanced over her shoulder toward the curtain barrier between us and Brie. When she swiveled her head back, her eyes sparked fire.

"Say whatever it is you've gotta say, Em." Doc pleaded, breaking the silence. He slung his arm around her shoulders, whether to comfort her or just feel something *good*, I had no idea.

"She's... It's like she's..." After several false starts, Emersyn got to the point. "That's not Brie in there."

"What do you mean?" Nell spoke up for the first time. "Of course it's Brie. Griff, you said it was her. I thought you found her!" Her accusing eyes bore into mine as tears rolled down her cheeks.

"Shhh, Half-pint," I crooned as I pulled Nell's body into mine. "It is Brie. I promise you, that is Brie in there."

Nell's shoulders shook with sobs. She wasn't normally so emotional, but the last seven months had taken a toll on all of us. I needed to remember that. I wasn't the only one affected by Brie's absence.

"Emersyn, please just explain what the fuck you meant!" Micah snapped, his frustration clear. It had to be killing him not to be here. We were all family, and Micah was usually the one giving orders and providing comfort. He had taken on that responsibility, and no matter how hard anyone tried to help, he never stopped.

"The Brie that is in that bay," Emersyn's thumb hitched over her shoulder, "that's not the Brie you all know and love. She still hasn't spoken and her face is devoid of all emotion. It's like someone turned off a light, and she stopped trying to turn it back on."

"Or she can't," I mumbled as I turned on my heel, determined to see her, consequences be damned.

"Griffin, wait!" Aiden's grip on my arm felt like a vice.

"You have five seconds to get your hand off me, Aiden," I threatened, my voice laced with steel.

"Griffin!" Micah snapped, loud enough that I forgot he wasn't really there.

"I need to see her! You don't understand. Please," I implored. "She's gonna need me, even more than before." The second the words passed my lips, I realized my mistake. I slammed my mouth shut, causing pain to radiate through my jaw. When Micah spoke, I thought I'd caught a break.

"And you'll get to see her once she's settled in a room. Let the doctors do their thing." Micah instructed. "Emersyn, is there anything else you can tell us?"

Emersyn shook her head in response before remembering that Micah couldn't see her.

"No. Not yet. I've asked the doctor to let me assist in her care, so I'll keep you updated as I know anything."

"You do that. And Emersyn," Micah's voice was strained, the gravity of the situation finally catching up to him. "Thank you."

"You're welcome." Emersyn kissed Doc on the cheek, and before she walked away, she turned to me and said, "I'll come get you when she's settled."

I didn't trust myself to speak, so I just nodded. I couldn't risk anyone asking me any questions. For years I'd kept her secret, and in a matter of seconds, I'd royally fucked up.

As I was walking away from the group, Micah's voice stopped me in my tracks.

"We'll discuss this later, Griff."

I stiffened at his words, my break over.

Fuck!

4

BRIE

My eyelids fluttered open and I rolled my head toward the voices in the room.

"So what you're saying is, she's going to need therapy?" I listened as Griffin spoke to the doctor, his forehead scrunching with the intensity of his concentration. Griffin was standing with his feet braced apart and his arms crossed over his chest. He looked intimidating, which was probably his intent. Griffin was nothing if not protective. Especially of me.

"Yes, therapy." The doctor pushed his glasses up his nose, and it appeared Griffin was getting to him. He was a short man with thinning hair, and his throat bobbed a few times as he swallowed, as if choosing his next words carefully. "I understand that she may be opposed to it, but I don't see any other way. She still hasn't spoken to anyone, and she's been here for three days. The trauma she's experienced, well," his shoulders shrugged and head shook before he continued, "we just don't know the extent of it."

Griffin glared at the man, and there was no mistaking the growl that he tried to silence. They still hadn't noticed I was awake, but as they continued discussing *my* trauma, my heartbeat quickened, triggering a cacophony of alarms to go off from all the machines around my bed. *They knew I was awake now.*

As they hurried to my bed, I rolled over, giving them my back. The beeping of the machines began to slow as I took several deep breaths to regulate my heart rate.

"What is that?" Griffin's voice came from behind me, and I tensed when his body jostled the bed.

"Just a low dose sedative to help Miss Coleman relax."

My body tensed, and the panic returned. As I peered over my shoulder at him, my eyes widened at the needle he held. He flicked the syringe to dissolve any air bubbles. Fire ants danced under my skin, and my breathing became erratic. Machines beeped chaotically, which only fueled my fear.

"Stop!" Griffin commanded and knocked the syringe out of the doctor's hand. The doctor froze, and if I hadn't been freaking out, I would have laughed at his expression. Mouth open, jaw slack. Utter confusion.

I couldn't get my panic under control. Griffin rolled me onto my back and grasped my chin, forcing me to look him in the eyes.

"I can help you. Do you want me to help you?" Griffin asked, his eyes seeking permission. In my head, I knew what he needed me to say but speech was impossible. I nodded frantically.

Griffin released my chin, and his left hand circled my throat as his right went to my hair and stroked. The hand on my throat squeezed, applying pressure to my carotid artery, and for a moment, the fear and panic was unbearable. Even more so than before I'd granted him permission to try to calm me.

"Do you trust me?"

I nodded and my vision became hazy as he applied more pressure.

"Good. That's a good girl," Griffin crooned. His eyes never left mine.

I was dimly aware of the doctor frantically racing to the door and yelling for security. I didn't care. Let them come.

The instruments monitoring my vitals slowly stopped their incessant chirping, and just as I was about to lose consciousness, Griffin released my neck. He stood still, his fierce gaze never wavering, his breathing choppy. I knew what that had cost him, and his dilating pupils confirmed it.

"Are you okay?" His voice was ragged, gravelly.

A single tear rolled down my cheek, and my head jerked from side to side. *No. I was not okay.* Griffin brushed the tear away with his thumb, and then quickly took a step back, chest heaving.

"What the hell was that?" The doctor's voice interrupted the moment, but I didn't care.

Griffin had eased my suffering the only way he knew how. I was grateful for it, but I hated that he would now have to explain something that was only ever meant to be between us.

"Nothing." Griffin held his body rigid, never turning to face the doctor.

"That most certainly was not 'nothing.'" The doctor huffed and scurried around to face the mountain of a man who was my savior. "That was assault."

That word was all it took for Griffin to snap.

"That was not assault!" Griffin grabbed the doctor by the lapels of his white coat and lifted him up so he had to stand on his tiptoes. "Does she look *assaulted* to you? You scared her, and I calmed her down. Simple as that."

"Griffin!" Aiden appeared, wrapping his arms around

Griffin from behind, trying to get him to release the doctor. "Let him go. Griffin, now!"

Griffin took a few deep breaths and slowly loosened his grip on the doctor. When he did, the doctor scrambled backward and almost fell. Aiden put a hand out to steady him before pulling Griffin to the door.

"Wait outside."

Aiden tried to push Griffin out the door, but he didn't budge. His gaze found mine, and I gave an almost imperceptible nod of my head. I didn't want him to leave, but even more than that, I didn't want him to get in trouble because of me.

"Please, Griff," Aiden begged. "I won't leave her alone with him." The doctor bristled at that, but Aiden didn't seem to notice or care. "I'll make sure she's okay."

"Fine." And with that, he was gone.

Without him in the room, my breathing once again became labored. The doctor came to the bed and pushed the call button. Within seconds a nurse in green scrubs entered the room.

"Yes, Dr. Shall?" the nurse asked as she turned the call light off.

"Please prepare another sedative for Miss Coleman."

"Right away," she responded and left the room.

"Miss Coleman," the doctor began, "I'm not going to hurt you. I'm going to give you a mild sedative so that you can relax. Maybe get some sleep, hmm?"

I shook my head from side to side and glanced toward Aiden, silently begging him to understand.

"Brie, please. Let Dr. Shall do his thing. He's not going to hurt you." Aiden pleaded with me. "You're safe here." His hand grazed my arm, and I flinched. Hurt crossed his features but he quickly masked it.

The nurse came back in the room with the sedative, and I

tried to roll away from her. Aiden's hand on my shoulder stopped me, and she injected the medicine into my IV. When she was done, I rolled over, silently cursing Aiden for allowing it.

"Thank you, Nurse Ross."

The nurse's retreating steps squeaked on cheap hospital tile after the doctor spoke.

"Brie, it's for your own good," Aiden whispered. "I'm sorry."

Betrayal washed over me as the medicine began to take effect. Voices faded and I surrendered to the drug.

5

GRIFFIN

"What the fuck was that, Griff?"

I didn't know how to answer that question, so I kept my mouth shut. I'd sat outside Brie's room and listened as Aiden let the doctor give her the sedative. I'd wanted to march back in there and kick his ass, but I refrained. He wasn't trying to hurt her, and besides, it wasn't his fault that he didn't know how to calm her down. That was a secret only I knew.

"Look, man," Aiden glared at me as he spoke, "I don't know what the hell that was all about, but you'd better start talking. I managed to convince the pissant doctor not to call the cops. For now. But he only agreed to that because I assured him you wouldn't be going back in that room." His head jerked toward the now closed door.

"Fuck that!" I roared, causing everyone in the hall to stop and stare.

Aiden grabbed my arm and tugged me closer to the wall.

"She needs me," I said in a more controlled tone.

"See, that's the thing." Aiden sighed and his brows dipped

in frustration. "You keep saying that, but why? She's going to need all of us, Griff. Not just you."

"I can't explain why. Can't you just trust me?"

"Jesus, I *do* trust you." Aiden shoved his fingers through his hair. "But this is ridiculous. You choked her! You get that that is ten kinds of fucked up, right?"

"I didn't choke her. I was helping her the only way I knew how. And you know what? It fucking worked."

This conversation was going nowhere. Fast. I couldn't give him answers. God knows I wanted to. *Needed* to. If for no other reason than to erase the unease and distrust that he was obviously experiencing. So, I tried a different tactic.

"She is going to need all of us. You're right about that. But I'm part of the 'all' in that statement."

"Fine. I'll see if Micah or Jackson can pull some strings." He started to walk away but stopped and looked over his shoulder. "Don't think I'm going to let this go. You're going to need to come clean about whatever the hell this is." And with that, he left.

I hung my head as I leaned back against the wall. *What a clusterfuck*. He was right, of course. But I would procrastinate as long as I could. It wasn't my story to tell, and I knew Brie was in no condition to clue them in.

I don't know how long I stood there. Thinking. Watching. Through one shift change, at least. Dr. Shall had left the room a while ago, staring daggers at me as he'd passed. My eyes burned, and my body was tired. I'd spent so much time and energy on finding Brie. Now that I knew she was safe, I was crashing.

"Here." Jackson stood in front of me and held out a chair. "Sit down before you fall over."

"Thanks," I mumbled, taking the chair from his hands and straddling it. "Who called you? Aiden or the doctor?"

"Neither." He chuckled. "I was already here when Micah called."

My eyes snapped to his. "Why?"

"Why was I here, or why did Micah call?"

"Both."

"I was here because I wanted to check in and see how Brie's doing. I was hoping she'd be awake so I could take her statement. And Micah called because he's worried about her." He paused and looked at me for a long moment. "And you."

"He doesn't need to worry about me. I'm fine."

"According to Aiden, that's not entirely true."

"I said, I'm fine. Let it go." I practically snarled at Jackson.

"Who are you trying to convince? All of us, or yourself?"

"Look, Jackson." I stood, knocking the chair over, and squared off with him. "You can't possibly understand. There are things…"

"Things?"

"Yes, things," I snapped. "What do you want from me?"

"How about the truth?"

I sighed and began to pace. I'd walked right into that one, and now I had to find a way to dig my way back out. Jackson picked up the chair and sat, waiting while I gathered my thoughts and debated on how much to say. With my mind made up, I stopped in front of him.

"Brie and I have a past, okay? Back when we were in boot camp, I helped her overcome some things." I refused to go into detail. Not here. Not now. Maybe not ever. "I know more about her than anyone else on the team, and she's made me promise, many times, not to tell anyone. I won't break that promise. Not for you and not for the BRB." I felt a little better getting even that little bit off my chest, but I still worried that I'd somehow betrayed Brie.

"Okay then." Jackson rested his hands on his knees and pushed himself up. "I'll go talk to the doctor and see if I can't convince him to let you stay. It's not like you're actually gonna leave anyway."

"Wait, that's it? No interrogation?"

"I don't know what you thought would happen but, no." He put his hand on my shoulder. "I trust you, Griffin. And so does everyone else. I just wish you trusted us as much." He dropped his hand and started to walk toward the elevator.

"Jackson?" I called when he'd gotten a few feet down the hall.

He turned back to me and crossed his arms over his chest. "What, Griffin?"

"I thought you were going to get a statement from Brie."

"I was, but she's asleep now. Besides, I think she's had an eventful enough day, don't you?" He didn't wait for my answer. He spun around and walked away. And I let him.

A few minutes after the elevator doors slid closed behind Jackson, Dr. Shall appeared and glared at me. I managed not to laugh because, really? He thought he could intimidate me? I was easily a foot taller than him and outweighed him by a good seventy-five pounds. Of muscle.

"Mr. Strong." I snickered as he said my name, causing him to square his shoulders. "I will allow—"

"I don't recall asking for your permission."

"I will allow you to stay here with Miss Coleman under two conditions."

"And what would those be?" I quirked my eyebrow. He was pissing me off, but I couldn't afford for him to kick me out for good.

"You will not interfere with her medical care. In *any* way." He took a deep breath before continuing. "Look, I don't approve of your *methods*, but they worked. If you can help with Miss Coleman's recovery, then I'm all for it. Quite frankly, in all my years of medical practice, I've never seen a case such as this."

Just as he finished talking, a security guard walked up behind him. His name badge read Waters.

"I suppose he's condition number two?" I nodded toward the guard.

"He is."

I was fuming and it must have showed in my rigid posture because Dr. Shall held up his hand to stop me from talking.

"While I can appreciate the bond you obviously have with Miss Coleman, I still have to ensure her safety." He paused, daring me with his eyes to say something. I remained silent. "I have spoken to the Sheriff, and he agrees that a guard, *outside the room*, is a good idea. I understand that the person who is responsible for her condition has not been arrested and it's a possibility that he could show up here."

As much as I hated to hear it, the little man had a point.

"Fine," I caved. As long as the guard wasn't in the room, I could deal with it. "And Dr. Shall?"

"Yes?"

"Thank you. You have my word. No harm will come to her, and as long as your medical care isn't scaring her, I'll stay out of your way."

"Not exactly the guarantee I was hoping for, but I suppose it'll have to do."

"Yes, it will, because it's the only one you're getting." I crossed my arms over my chest and dared him to challenge me.

"Well, then." He cleared his throat. "I'll have a cot brought into the room. I assume you'll be staying until she's released?"

"Damn straight."

"Okay. My shift is over," he glanced at his watch, "in half an hour. I'll leave my contact information at the nurses' station in case you or Miss Coleman need anything. If there's nothing else?"

"I'm good."

"Good evening, Mr. Strong."

"Night, doc."

After Dr. Shall left, I remained outside the door for several minutes, Waters and I swapping evil eyes.

"You got a problem?" He asked me.

"No problem here. Just do your job and let me do mine and we'll get along just fine."

"And what would that be? Your job, I mean."

"To protect Brie. At all costs." I turned and walked into the room before shutting the door in Waters's face.

I scrubbed my hands over my face as I leaned back against the door. A few seconds later, there was a soft knock and I turned to open it.

"Yes?" I snapped, thinking it was the guard.

"Dr. Shall asked me to bring this in for you, Mr. Strong." The nurse's eyes darted toward the floor, and I felt bad for having scared her.

"Thank you," I said and relieved her of the contraption. I shut the door, not even giving her a chance to respond. I was too damn tired to drag out the pleasantries and way past the point of caring.

I turned around and froze when my gaze landed on Brie.

What the hell is wrong with you?

I forced my feet to move and walked farther into the room. I set up the cot and plopped down. *Damn, I'm tired.* Bracing my arms across my forehead, I allowed my thoughts to drift back to when I'd first met Brie, at boot camp.

6

GRIFFIN

10 years earlier...

"Drop and give me twenty!" Recruit Division Commander Johnson demanded of us new recruits.

It was week two of boot camp at the Great Lakes Naval Training Center and we'd already lost seven recruits. As RDC Johnson walked around and watched us struggle, I couldn't help the pride that surged through me. My form was perfect, and twenty push-ups wouldn't even cause me to break a sweat.

"Is there a problem, recruit?" RDC Johnson bent down to the guy next to me and got right in his face. This particular recruit was a pansy and would likely be the next to fail. His breathing was ragged. His arms shook and sweat trickled down his face.

"Sir, no sir," he responded, picking up his pace.

"Make it fifty!" RDC Johnson shouted as he stood.

"Asshole," the recruit on my other side mumbled. I hadn't thought it was loud enough for the RDC to hear, but I was wrong.

"What's that, princess?" RDC Johnson was right in her face and spit flew from his mouth as he yelled.

"Sir, nothing sir," she responded, her voice barely above a whisper.

"Louder, princess!"

"Sir, nothing sir." Her voice was louder, but it shook.

What the hell?

I chanced a look in her direction and almost forgot what I was doing. *Damn.* She was dressed in the same navy blue sweats as everyone else, but she made them look good. The gold 'Navy' emblazoned on the chest rippled as her breasts heaved with exertion. Her ebony hair was in a ponytail and slicked with sweat, but that didn't detract from her beauty. In fact, it enhanced it, and I found myself wishing I had a better view of her face.

"That's what I thought," he said, pulling me from my admiration. He moved on to his next victim, leaving her to survive another day.

"What are you looking at?" The woman snapped at me.

"Nothing." Heat crept up my neck at having been caught. "I'm Griffin." I continued my push-ups.

"Brie," she huffed.

"Don't let him get to you. It's his job to make us miserable."

She stiffened at my words, and I immediately regretted them.

"I don't recall giving you permission to speak, princess!" RDC Johnson was back, and this time, he'd planted his foot on her back to keep her from completing her push-up.

I watched as her eyes became wide as saucers and her

breathing became choppy. I glared at the RDC but didn't speak, not wanting to jeopardize myself. It was a war I fought from within because I wanted to punch the prick's lights out. He recognized the shift in her breathing, and rather than make sure she was okay, he pushed down harder with his boot.

"Aww, do you need to call Daddy? Would he make it all better for you?" he taunted.

Brie took several steadying breaths, and I watched in horror as a tear dripped to the asphalt.

I fucking lost my shit.

"Get off her." I jumped to my feet, my hands balling into fists at my sides. Rage boiled my blood and rushed to my face.

"Excuse me?" He didn't even have the decency to look at me when he spoke.

"I said, 'get off her.'"

"I don't recall asking for your opinion." He finally shifted his attention to me, and when he did, he removed his foot from her back.

Brie immediately swiped at the wetness on her cheek and resumed her push-ups. The instructor was spewing venom about knowing my place, but I didn't care. I was fascinated by her ability to mask whatever emotion she had been feeling not two minutes ago.

"And I don't recall the part where we were told it was okay for an RDC to inflict pain on a recruit." My chest was heaving with equal parts anger and fear. Anger at the asshole standing in front of me and fear because that same asshole held my future in his hands and I'd just stepped in a heaping pile of shit.

"What's your name, recruit?"

"Griffin Strong." I realized too late that I'd responded in a manner that would only cause me more trouble.

"Excuse me?" The vein in RDC Johnson's neck bulged and his face reddened in anger.

"Sir, Griffin Strong, sir." It was time to start digging myself out of this pile. I accomplished what I set out to accomplish. Brie was no longer his focus and she needed to stop being mine.

"You've earned yourself watch duty with Chief Petty Officer Mallory tonight. Report to him at zero hundred hours. You will stay on watch duty until zero six hundred hours, at which time, you will report to me. Do you understand?"

"With all due—"

"You just earned yourself that schedule for a week, recruit!"

"Sir, yes, sir." I was angry, not stupid. Sleep deprivation was no joke, and RDC Johnson was determined to make me suffer.

"Good." He smirked and I knew he wasn't done doling out consequences. "Drop and give me a hundred."

I dropped and began my push-ups. When I was ten push-ups in, RDC Johnson upped the ante.

"On second thought," he turned toward Brie, "Princess, on Recruit Strong's back. Now!"

Brie flinched, almost imperceptibly, but she stood up and wiped her palms down her thighs. I watched as she took a few steps towards me and stopped.

"What are you waiting for? On his back!" RDC Johnson grabbed her bicep and jerked her closer to me until her shins hit my body.

Brie lowered her body to mine until her entire front was pressed against my back. She trembled, causing my body to vibrate. *Why is she shaking?* She wasn't the one who was going to have to do ninety push-ups with a tense female on board.

"What the hell were you thinking?" Brie fiercely whispered in my ear after I resumed my push-ups. "I didn't need your help."

I ignored her question, not wanting to call her out on her bullshit. Something had flashed through her mind when RDC Johnson called her princess, and I was determined to figure out what that was. No need to alienate her by being an asshole now.

Her shaking had slowed to a sporadic tremble, and the longer she was on my back, the harder it became to focus on the task at hand. Her weight felt good. Too good. My mind wandered, thinking about what her trembling would feel like if she were pressed up against me for pleasure.

Within seconds of completing the hundredth push-up, Brie's weight disappeared. I let my arms go slack, causing my chest to hit the ground. I stayed there for a minute, forcing myself to think about something other than the boner-inducing fantasies I'd been imagining. Once I felt confident I could stand without embarrassing myself, I jumped up and faced Brie. She was staring past me, mixed emotions crossing her face.

"Brie?" I asked.

Her eyes flashed to mine and she quickly schooled her expression.

"Next time, stay out of it." She snapped before turning and walking away.

Stay out of it? *Not a chance in hell.*

7

BRIE

Present day...

"You ready to go in?" Griffin asked, after parking the car in front of the main house.

I vigorously shook my head. My palms were sweaty and my heartbeat was climbing at an alarming rate. Talking was still impossible. Not because I didn't want to. I wanted to, more than anything. I just… couldn't.

"Okay. We can sit here as long as you need to."

I'd been itching to get out of the hospital after having been there for two weeks. But at least there, the medications they'd pumped into me had kept me numb. I hadn't been able to think. Or remember. Now, without the drugs coursing through my system, I remembered everything. And it was too much.

"Brie?" Griffin's voice filtered in, mixing with the other voice I couldn't get rid of. "Brie, look at me."

BROKEN INNOCENCE

I raised my eyes to him, feeling the tears slipping down my cheeks, hating myself for the weakness.

"What can I do?"

I shrugged and focused on my hands in my lap. Griffin's hand came into view, and I flinched. He didn't let that stop him from picking up my hand and rubbing soothing circles over my wrist. Watching his thumb go back and forth over my healing cuts was hypnotic. I wasn't sure how long we sat in silence, but I was grateful he didn't ask questions about the wounds.

"Why don't we go to your cabin? You can visit with everyone else when you're ready."

I inhaled deeply and nodded. Leave it to Griffin to know exactly what I needed, while I didn't have a fucking clue.

"Okay. Let me run in and let everyone know so they don't worry." With that said, he left me alone in the car.

Guilt nagged at me as I waited for him to come back. The 'everyone' he referred to were my friends. My family. I should be excited to see them. Happy to be home. But I wasn't. Instead, I felt... empty.

I jumped at the sound of the car door being opened. My bottom lip quivered, and my brow furrowed when Griffin looked at me.

"They aren't mad, so get that look off your face. They want to see you. Spend time with you. But they understand." He glanced out the window toward the house. He was gripping the steering wheel, and I knew him well enough to know he was trying to sort out something in his head.

"Ready?" He loosened his grip and turned the car on.

I wasn't, so I turned to peer out the window. Truth was, I didn't want to be anywhere on the property, but this was my home and I was going to have to face it at some point. Might as well be now, while I had Griffin for support.

Griffin sighed as he put the car in gear and pressed the gas. As he drove to my cabin, I chewed my lower lip and watched as we passed trees that I'd seen a million times before. Everything looked the same, but felt different. The last time I'd been at my cabin, it'd been with Ian. He'd picked me up to go to the main house for the Labor Day barbeque and I'd been giddy with excitement. Not to see Ian. He had been a distraction, nothing more. I'd been looking forward to spending time with everyone without everyday life getting in the way.

"We're here." Griffin's voice pulled me from my musings.

He got out and walked around to open my door for me. Griffin has always been a gentleman, despite his rough exterior. He had more reason than most to hate me, but he didn't and I had no idea why. All my efforts to push him away, even as far back as boot camp, were met with nothing but kindness and a loyalty I didn't deserve.

"You coming?" He held out his hand for me.

Ignoring his hand, I got out of the car. Griffin frowned at me and I had to look away. I lifted my hand to shield my eyes from the sun as he retrieved my bag, as well as another, from the backseat. The second bag didn't look familiar, and my panic started to surface again.

My eyebrows pinched together, and I looked at him in confusion.

"It's my go-bag," he said, referring to the bag we all had packed so we were ready to go at a moment's notice. "I'm staying with you."

My eyes widened in surprise, but he said nothing more. He started toward the porch, and after climbing the steps, he turned back to see me rooted in the same spot.

"Brie." He jogged back down the steps. "Come on. It's getting late and you need to take your meds." He was referring to the Vicodin I was prescribed for pain, as well as Amoxicillin, Zoloft, and Ambien. The doctor had said I shouldn't be alone while on so many medications, but I hadn't expected Griffin to be the one to stay with me. Nell or Sadie, maybe, but not Griffin.

I shuffled my feet in the dirt driveway. My breathing was ragged and sweat began to bead on my forehead. Griffin was beside me in an instant, gray eyes flashing. They reminded me of a summer storm. I'd seen that look before, and its cause was worry.

"Breathe, baby," Griffin crooned as he rubbed circles on my back. "Just breathe. I know you'd probably rather have Sadie or Nell here, but you're stuck with me." He chuckled to soften the news. "Sadie has the babies and Nell has a date with Jake."

As he spoke, I focused on my breathing and his tone. It didn't matter what he said. Whatever it was, he was calming me. When my panic seemed to subside, Griffin stepped away from me, forever patient.

We stood there for a few more minutes before he wrapped his fingers around my arm and nudged me forward. I flinched when his hand made contact, but he refused to budge. He simply pulled out his key and unlocked the door. When he swung it open, his hand grazed the small of my back, guiding me over the threshold. I waited for the crushing panic to surface, but it didn't. *Maybe this won't be so bad.*

"I'm gonna put your stuff in your room."

Griffin disappeared from view, and I walked farther into my living room. *Familiar, yet so different.* There were pictures on the walls of the entire BRB. Some were from overseas, all of us dressed in fatigues. Some were from boot camp and others were more recent. My eyes zeroed in on the one of Griffin and me at some dive bar in Michigan.

The photo so clearly captured how I had felt that night. I'd gone to the bar after a particularly infuriating phone call from my uncle, who blamed me for… everything. At the time, drinking my problems away had seemed like the perfect solution. I'd had no idea Griffin would be there, and when I saw him, my stomach had bottomed out. My first instinct had been to run like hell because I hadn't had to face him since the incident at the beginning of boot camp. He hadn't commented on it, but I knew he'd seen my fear that day.

"Man, that was a good night." Griffin's rough timbre was right behind me. *How had I not heard him coming?*

I turned away from the photo and walked toward the couch, not acknowledging what he'd said because he was right. It had been a good night. It was the night Griffin taught me how to feel without fear. More than that, he taught me how to do the one thing I'd never learned. He taught me to trust.

8

BRIE

10 years earlier...

The guy from boot camp stalked toward me, determination in his stride. The rest of the crowd at the Quarterdeck fell away, and I almost forgot my reason for coming to the bar. Fuck, he was hot. I'd noticed his looks the first time I'd seen him, but hadn't truly been able to appreciate them, under the circumstances. The tingle between my legs told me just how much I appreciated them now.

He was dressed in a black T-shirt that fit him like a second skin and showed off his impressive biceps. His jeans were faded, and his thigh muscles flexed as he walked. My eyes roamed over his magnificent physique and landed on his boots. They were black riding boots. I knew this because they were similar to my own. The ones I wore when I rode Chaos, my Harley Davidson Street Glide.

"My eyes are up here, Brie." I slowly raised my head. He was standing right in front of me. So close.

"Griffin, right?" I forced myself to speak past the lust and fear. Looking at his face sent fire through my belly. His eyes were gray, like a thunder cloud, and they currently held a look of amusement.

He was a big man. Strong, intimidating. I'd dealt with strong and intimidating my entire life, and it always ended with me feeling nothing but fear, so it didn't surprise me that I felt it now. The lust, though... that was new.

"Right. But you can call me Griff." He had a killer smile and no doubt it had won over many women. "Or handsome, stud, sexy... really anything you like."

"How 'bout asshole? That seems to fit you perfectly." My voice sounded far more cocky than I felt, but my nerves were beginning to settle. I crossed my arms over my chest, which pushed my breasts out, drawing his gaze.

"My eyes are up here, *asshole.*"

"Touché." Griffin chuckled and returned his stare to my face. "So, Brie, what brings you here?"

"I imagine the same thing as everyone else." My response was clipped, but I didn't care. No way was I telling him what had driven me to seek out alcohol-induced oblivion.

"Well, then, let's get you—"

I marched past him and straight up to the bar, not giving a damn what he had to say.

"Double shot of Jack, please," I spoke to the bartender, ignoring the eyes boring into my back. The amber liquid burned as I threw my head back and downed it in one gulp.

I slammed my shot glass down on the bar. "Two more."

"Coming right up." The bartender lined up the shot glasses.

"Put it on my tab, Jim."

I whirled around and shot daggers at Griffin, who was

standing a little too close. I backed up until the bar dug into my spine. I loathed the automatic response, but it had been ingrained in me since I was a little girl. I was getting better but not fast enough.

"No, Jim." I spoke to the man behind the bar, but my gaze never wavered from Griffin. "I pay my own way."

"It's just a drink, Brie." Griffin's face was blank, but something in his eyes flashed.

"Yeah, until it's not," I mumbled, looking at the floor.

For several seconds, my pounding heart and Griffin's breathing were the only sounds that registered. When I trusted myself enough to lift my head, what I saw scared the shit out of me. Griffin's face was set in stone, and his gray eyes swirled with anger.

"Who hurt you?" Steel laced the question.

"What?" I was surprised that he'd picked up on that, though I shouldn't have been. He didn't strike me as someone who missed much.

"You heard me." He must have sensed my apprehension because his features softened the tiniest bit. There was also a bit of pity written on his face, which caused my anger to resurface.

"No one," I bit out and turned away from him.

His hand snaked out and he gripped my arm, forcing me to turn around and face him.

"Don't lie to me, Brie."

"Get your hand off of me!" My chest was heaving with a mixture of anger and anxiety. I didn't like to be touched, especially by a brute who thought he held power over me.

He didn't release my arm, but his grasp loosened.

"Who. Hurt. You?"

I yanked out of his hold, turned to down my other two shots, and slapped money on the bar. Before the burning liquid had a chance to settle, I pushed past Griffin and didn't stop until I was outside standing next to Chaos. I knew I should call a cab, but I also craved an ending to my pain.

I straddled Chaos but didn't turn him on. A large part of me wanted to get the hell out of there, consequences be damned, but another part of me knew I wasn't ready to die. *Fuck that!* I wouldn't give my memories the satisfaction.

"Going somewhere?"

I stood and turned toward the deep voice on the sidewalk.

"Fuck you!" I raged. It infuriated me that he could be so calm when my brain was waging a war.

"I'm sorry if I scared you." He sounded genuine, but I couldn't be sure.

"I'm not scared." I sounded like a petulant child. I stood up straighter and squared my shoulders. "I just don't like being touched."

"Fair enough." He put his hands up in front of him, in a gesture of surrender. He stood just like that for several long moments, almost as if he was waiting for me to relax. Somehow, his patience calmed me slightly and my tightly wound muscles began to uncoil.

"Truce?" He stuck his hand out and my eyes dropped from his face to stare at it. Tentatively, I grasped his hand and shook. "Truce."

Before I could read too much into the electricity that buzzed through my system, I let go. I walked past him to go back inside, ignoring his chuckle.

Griffin's heat surrounded me as he was forced to walk right at my back through the crowd. Ribbons of fire curled through my body, but they weren't from fear. They were something I'd never experienced before...*desire*. I didn't even think I was capable of the feeling.

A flash caught my attention, and I snapped my head

toward its source. Griffin reached out and snatched the phone from the guy who'd taken the picture.

"What the hell?" Picture Guy spoke, but he sounded more amused than mad.

"Screw off, Aiden." Griffin laughed.

"You know him?" I asked Griffin.

"Brie, this is Aiden. Utter pain in my ass." There was no heat in his words, so I assumed the two were friends. "Aiden, meet Brie."

"Wait, Brie? As in, 'the most beautiful woman I've ever seen' Brie?" Aiden clutched his chest, mocking Griffin.

"The most beautiful woman you've ever seen, huh?" I turned toward Griffin, enjoying the flush that crept up his neck. My fear and anger vanished, and I found myself enjoying their back and forth banter.

"I'm deleting this picture," Griffin grumbled, ignoring my question.

"Wait!" I grabbed the phone from Griffin's hand and looked at the photo on the screen.

His brows rose in question, and I could understand his confusion. My emotions were all over the place, and I certainly wasn't doing anything to clear them up for him.

I licked my lips before trying to explain. "Um... I'll delete it. I, uh, I don't trust you."

Aiden had captured the perfect moment, and I wanted it. The image didn't show my anger, my fear. It didn't look like two people who barely knew one another. The moment that was frozen in time was... intimate. And I needed it.

I quickly forwarded the image to myself and then hit delete a split second before the device was ripped from my hands. Aiden turned his back on Griffin and me and headed toward the bar.

"You coming?" He glanced back at us and bobbed his eyebrows suggestively.

"Like I said, pain in my ass." Exasperation tinged Griffin's words, but he was grinning as he spoke.

Griffin sauntered away, and I allowed myself a moment to enjoy the view. He really was incredibly built. He leaned on the bar, causing his shirt to stretch across his back and heat to pool in my belly. I mentally fanned myself and forced my feet to carry me to the bar.

"Shot for the lady, Jim," Aiden said.

"Thanks, Aiden."

"Seriously?" Griffin crossed his arms over his chest. "You nearly took my head off when I tried to pay for your drinks earlier."

"Truce, remember?" I responded with sugary sweetness. I was finally having a good time, and I refused to let him ruin it.

"Fine, but the next one's on me."

"Whatever." I winced as my childish tone grated like fingernails on a chalkboard.

"So, Brie, what brings you to Quarterdeck?" Aiden asked.

I hesitated to answer because Griffin had asked me the same thing and I'd given him shit for it. I stuck to the same answer, not wanting to cause any friction.

"Same thing as everyone else. To drink." I reached around Aiden to grab my shot off the bar and downed it in one long gulp.

"Smart ass," Griffin teased. He downed his shot and the slam of his glass on the bar caused me to jump.

"You okay?" Aiden asked me as he picked up his drink.

"Sure. Never better." I forced a tight smile, took his glass out of his hand, and downed it.

"Whoa, slow down, Brie." Griffin had a worried look on his face.

I ignored his instruction and ordered another drink—Jack and Coke.

"Make it two, Jim. And put them on my tab." I stiffened at Griffin's words but let it go.

"I'll make sure you get home." Griffin leaned in and whispered in my ear. "You can keep chasing away your demons."

My eyes snapped to his, and in that moment, one thing became crystal clear.

When it came to Griffin Strong, I was fucked.

9

GRIFFIN

Bloop... bloop... bloop...

The dripping faucet made it almost impossible to sleep. Not that I would have anyway. Brie had insisted every light in the house be left on, and we were lit up like a fucking Christmas tree.

It was only eleven o'clock, but Brie had been in bed since nine. She still hadn't spoken to me, and I found myself craving the sound of her voice. It wouldn't matter what she said. Hell, she could call me an asshole a million times and I wouldn't care. As long as she was talking.

My cell phone buzzed in my shorts.

"Yo." I answered as quietly as I could so I didn't wake Brie. At least one of us needed to sleep.

"Griff, how is she?" Micah made no effort to be quiet, telling me he was likely at the main house and not with Sadie and the twins.

Unsure how to answer that, I blew out a breath. As I gathered my thoughts, I walked to the back door to step outside.

"Well?" Micah was not the most patient man to begin with and certainly not when he was pissed off. I knew he hadn't forgotten what Jackson told him about the hospital. He'd granted me a reprieve for the two weeks Brie had remained there, but, with her home, he wanted answers.

"I don't even know, man. It's like she's here, but she's not. Ya know?" I wasn't sure how to explain it without going into more than I had a right to.

"Yeah. Yeah, I get it. Has she told you anything yet?"

"Nothing." I pictured Brie sitting at the table after I made dinner. She'd looked so lost. She'd even flinched when I went to pick her plate up to carry it to the sink. Anger spiked at the memory. "I need to know what happened! I need her to talk! I need—"

"What you need is to calm the fuck down," Micah snapped. "This isn't about what you need. Jesus, Griff. Your temper is not what *she* needs!"

"Fuck!" My fist connected with the railing of the back porch and pain shot up my arm.

"Look, I'm going to send Doc up there. You don't need to be around her right now."

"I'm not leaving," I growled.

"You'll do as you're ordered."

I'd never resisted Micah's orders before. I'd always followed him. Agreed with him. But not this time. Not when he didn't know everything.

"Man, please. Give me time. You know I'd never take my temper out on her." Begging felt foreign to me.

"Really? Is that why you choked her?"

And there it was. The reason for his anger. His distrust of me.

"You have no fucking clue what you're talking about."

"So Jackson got it wrong? The doctor didn't see you with your hands wrapped around her throat?" I knew what he wanted to hear, but I couldn't lie. Not to him.

"There's more to it than that." My fingers wound threw

my hair in frustration. I knew what was coming, and I was helpless to stop it.

"Well, then, enlighten me."

As I was about to respond, a shadow appeared through the curtain. Brie was up, and that was my cue to cut this short.

"Tomorrow. Send Nell up here to sit with Brie, and I'll come to the main house in the morning," I whispered as my eyes tracked Brie's every move.

"Fine. Nine o'clock?"

"I'll be there." I hit the end button and went inside, already dreading the morning.

⁓

Micah sat at the desk, leaning back in his chair with his arms folded over his chest. Normally he wouldn't have intimidated me, but this morning, he did.

My mouth was full of cotton, and I reached for the Gatorade I'd snagged from the refrigerator. I took a swig of the cold liquid and tried to gather my thoughts. Micah stared at me, no doubt waiting for me to speak first.

"Spill it, Griff." I guess he was done waiting.

"It's not my story to tell."

"I don't give a damn!" His palms slammed down on the desk as he rose from his chair. He leaned across and spoke through gritted teeth. "You said you'd explain, so start explaining."

I stood up and started to pace, beating a path across the library floor. After several minutes, and long suffering sighs from my best friend, I took him back to the beginning.

"Do you remember the night we met? Back when I was assigned watch duty with you?" I stopped pacing and plopped into the chair, forcing myself to meet his eyes.

"Of course I do. You were a cocky bastard, but Johnson was a prick," he snorted. "I can't believe he crossed that line with a female recruit. He'd always rubbed me the wrong way, but I never thought—"

I saw in his eyes the moment Micah realized who the female recruit was. I'd never told him because I didn't want to cause her any embarrassment.

"Brie?" He asked.

I nodded and swallowed the apology that was on the tip of my tongue. I had nothing to be sorry for. Other than the fact that I'd kept secrets from my best friend—the one who had never kept a secret from me.

"Okay. That still doesn't explain what you did at the hospital."

"I helped her!" I jumped up and leaned across the desk, coming to within an inch of his face. He didn't even have the decency to flinch.

"Sit. Down." Micah enunciated.

I sat down with a thud, the front feet of the chair coming off the floor.

"Griffin, you've got two options. You can either calm the fuck down and tell me whatever it is you think is going to make what you did okay, or," voice grating, Micah continued, "you can get the hell off BRB property until option one sounds better."

"You can't kick me out."

"Try me." Eyebrows raised, Micah placed the proverbial ball squarely in my court.

We stared at each other for several minutes before I realized I didn't have a choice. I was going to talk, and Micah knew it. What he didn't know was what I was risking.

"Six months after we met, Brie showed up at the Quarterdeck with a chip on her shoulder." I walked Micah through

Brie's past, hating myself a little more with every word that came out of my mouth.

10

GRIFFIN

10 years earlier...

"So, Brie." Aiden leaned into her to be heard over the music. "Where ya from?"

I wanted to punch him. He knew I was interested. Shit, I'd staked my claim six months ago when I'd first met her. The only thing that kept my fist from connecting with his face was the fear she'd shown earlier. Fear was not a response I was hoping to elicit from her.

"New York." Uncertainty crept into her eyes. "The Bronx." She turned on her stool to look out at the crowd. The Quarterdeck had filled up fast in the last hour, and with the addition of every new patron, Brie's face displayed more and more anxiety.

"You okay?" I placed my hand on her upper back, and she flinched.

"Oh, um, yeah. I'm good," she mumbled. She tossed back

another shot of Jack Daniels. I'd lost count a while ago of how many she'd had.

She scooted off her stool and stumbled. My arms shot out to catch her, and in the process, her shirt rose, baring tanned flesh. Little scars marred her flat stomach. *Cigarette burns?*

My brain told me to let go, but my hands had a mind of their own. My eyes shot to hers, and her panic registered. After I was sure she wasn't going to fall on her ass, I let go and watched as she smoothed her shirt back into place.

"I have to go," she muttered. She scurried through the bar as fast as she could, only to be stopped by a pretty boy in chinos right before making it out the door.

I pushed through the crowd while I watched Pretty Boy snake his arm around her waist. She tried to slap his hands away, but she was no match for him.

Several drunk sailors got in my way and slowed me down. I was close enough to hear some of their exchange, though. Just not close enough to strangle the bastard.

"Leave me alone," she cried.

"Come on, babe. You're practically begging for it in those jeans." He leaned in and shoved his tongue in her mouth.

She pushed at his body and struggled against the arms banded around her.

"Ow!" He suddenly pulled away from her, and I was struck with a mixture of satisfaction and regret. Satisfaction at the blood dripping from his mouth and regret that I hadn't been the one to make him bleed.

"Crazy bitch!" Time seemed to stop as he drew his hand back and swung it across her cheek.

"Hey fucker!" I yelled, drawing his attention. I was finally right behind him, and the moment he turned around, my fist connected with his face, knocking his ass to the ground. Adrenaline surged through me as the sound of bone crunching reached my ears. My chest heaved as I stared at his motionless form. My hands itched to hit him again, but it wouldn't have been a fair fight.

"Dude, she's getting away." Aiden's voice penetrated the rage, and I looked up to see Brie shoving her way through the door. She stumbled to the bike she'd been about to leave on earlier.

"Brie!" I shouted, running after her. "Brie, wait!"

I reached her as the bike roared to life and jumped in front of it before she had a chance to take off.

"Move. Now!" She wasn't wearing a helmet, and her ebony hair blew in the night breeze, showing off her slender neck. Lust shot through me like lightning, and I took a few deep breaths to control it.

"You're drunk."

Her eyes were luminous pools of liquid gold, and she'd captured her bottom lip between her teeth, no doubt to stop the trembling. It was sexy as fuck.

"At least let me drive you home." I let my muscles relax and grinned, hoping to ease some of the tension that was coiling through her.

She looked around and didn't speak. Her forehead wrinkled, making me think she was trying to determine if there was any way around accepting my offer.

"Please," I pleaded. "Consider it a favor. I'll feel better knowing you got home safe. Otherwise, I'll lose sleep because I'll worry and then dickhead Johnson will ride my ass tomorrow because I'll be too tired to do a damn thing."

She still didn't speak, but her lips quirked up into the slightest grin. The tension lifted and the small smile morphed into a full belly laugh. My breath caught at the way her face lit up. She was beautiful no matter what, but when she smiled, she was stunning.

"What about Chaos?" she asked when she got control of herself.

"Who's Chaos?" Jealousy settled like a lead weight in my gut.

"The bad boy I'm straddling." She ran her hands over the chrome handlebars. I wanted to be on the receiving end of her caress more than I wanted my next breath.

"I'll make sure to bring you back to get your bike."

"Chaos." Her eyes narrowed as she corrected me.

"Chaos," I repeated, the corner of my mouth lifting into a smile.

What Brie didn't know was that I had Amina, my Harley-Davidson Fat Boy. I couldn't wait to see the look on her face when she saw her. She clearly appreciated beauty, and Amina was about as close to perfection as a bike could get.

Just then, Pretty Boy walked out of the bar and came right for us. I stepped back up on the curb, blocking Brie. Arms crossed over my chest, legs braced apart, I glared at him.

"Better walk the other way," I snarled, almost wishing he wouldn't. He wasn't going to give me what I wanted, though. He stopped and stared at me, weighing his options.

"Let's go." Brie's body pressed against mine from behind.

I stepped to the side and wrapped my arm around her, pulling her into my side. Her hand came around me, and her fingers dug into my abs. Pretty Boy looked like he wanted to follow us as I led her away, but he wisened up and went back into the Quarterdeck.

Never taking my arm away, I guided Brie toward Amina. That was the longest block and a half of my life. I recited the National Anthem in my head, hoping to cool the heat in my blood. Her body was perfection against mine, and I longed to claim her. Show her that not all men craved inflicting pain. Because she had definitely experienced pain. I wanted, no *needed*, to show her that she could experience pleasure with the right man. With me.

"This is yours?" A smile bloomed on her face when we reached Amina.

"Yep. Amina," I proudly responded.

"Damn," she breathed. Her hands ran over Amina in admiration. "I mean, I knew you had a bike, but this? I didn't expect this."

"How'd you know?" My eyebrow quirked, and she glanced down at my boots. I chuckled, realizing that they were a dead giveaway to anyone who knew anything about bikes and riding.

She stepped away from Amina and fidgeted with her hands while glancing up and down the street.

I took a chance and gripped her chin, forcing her to look at me. She didn't flinch. Instead, her pupils dilated and that told me everything I needed to know. She was starting to trust me, and more importantly, some part of her wanted what I had to offer. As long as she felt safe.

"What's wrong, Brie?" My voice dipped low and dripped with a heady mixture of hunger and concern.

"Nothing. I, um…" She licked her lips before she continued. "I'm not ready to go home." Her eyes lowered as she spoke, and my cock strained painfully against my zipper.

"What do you want, Brie?" I prayed she wanted the same thing I did.

Her eyes begged me not to make her answer that, but I needed her to. She had to know that this was her choice, and I needed to hear the words. I leaned in and let my breath caress her cheek, her ear.

"Tell me," I whispered.

"You."

She shivered with that one word. My first instinct was to throw her on Amina and race like hell to get her to my bed, but I discarded that thought. Brie had shown so much fear, despite her trying so hard to hide it. She required care and patience.

Framing her face in my hands, I touched my forehead to hers.

"Do you trust me?"

"Yes. No. I don't know." She wrinkled her nose in an adorable way.

"You will."

I brushed my lips against hers, needing the contact. She melted into me as I pulled away. I handed her my helmet and waited as she secured the strap under her chin. After I climbed on Amina, Brie straddled the bike, and her thighs hugged mine.

This was going to be a long ride home.

∼

Anticipation overwhelmed me as I pulled into the driveway of the one-story ranch house I rented. Most new recruits weren't permitted to live off base, but I'd worked my way up in rank and moved in a week ago.

As I parked Amina, Brie's arms loosened, and she pulled away from me. I remained on the bike while she took her helmet off. I didn't trust myself to stand with the raging hard-on I was sporting.

"Griffin?" Brie stood in front of me with a quizzical look on her face.

Determined to not make her wait, I stood up and swung my leg over the seat. As I turned to rest the helmet on the bike, I adjusted myself.

"Let's go." I threw my arm around her shoulders and steered her toward the porch.

After pushing open the front door, I stepped aside to let Brie enter first. She glanced at me, uncertainty entering her eyes. Gone was the spark of fire I'd seen earlier. In its place was fear. I had to get this turned around. Quick.

"I'm not him." Gravel laced my tone as anger mixed with need.

Her eyes widened, and her pupils dilated. Most people would have missed that tell-tale sign of arousal, but I wasn't most people.

"I'm sorry," she mumbled as she shook her head. "I, um, don't normally do this." Her lashes lowered and a faint blush crept into her cheeks.

"Look at me," I commanded.

Her eyes snapped to mine, and the blush darkened to crimson. *Perfect.*

"Let me show you how good letting go can be." I placed my finger on her lips when they parted to interrupt me. "This stops the second you say 'no'. I can make you soar if you let me."

My hand fell to my side when I was done speaking. I'd said all I could at this point. How she chose to proceed would tell me just how ready she was to let her guard down.

"Okay." She spoke so quietly I had to strain to hear her.

I bent my knees so I was eye level with her. The gold flecks in her irises caught the porch light, reminding me of rings of fire. My cock swelled, and my heart thundered. Possessiveness warred with protectiveness, and for the first time, possessiveness wasn't winning.

"I know something happened to you and whatever it was, I'm sorry." I never broke eye contact as I spoke, needing her to see *me* and not whoever had made her this way. "If we get inside and you decide that all you want is to talk, then I'll listen to every word. But I know you want this as much as I do. It's up to you whether it happens tonight or another time. And before you make a decision, remember this. I'm. Not. Him."

Brie took a deep breath and blew it out slowly. She looked over my shoulder into the living room and brushed past me. Her boots thudded on the hardwood floor, and the couch sank under her weight as she plopped down.

"Can I get you a drink?" I walked past her into the kitchen. I made sure she stayed in my line of sight and I in hers. No sense in giving her the opportunity to flee. Not when I knew I could help her. Heal her.

"Beer, if you've got it."

I strode back into the living room carrying the six-pack of Tilted Earth I'd grabbed from the fridge. When I sat down next to her, our thighs touched. I handed her a bottle of the brew after twisting the cap off and flipping it onto the coffee table. She took a long pull from the frosted bottle, and I was captivated at the sight of her lips wrapped around the top.

Brie guzzled her first drink down and reached for a second. I was only halfway through my first by the time she polished off that one. I didn't try to stop her or slow her down. If this was what she needed to relieve some of the tension that was visible in her posture, then I'd let her drink.

"Can I tell you something?" she whispered, after finishing her third beer.

"If you want to."

My fingers grazed her cheek and slid an errant strand of hair behind her ear. She shivered at the contact.

"I, uh..." she paused and audibly swallowed. "I'm scared."

"Of me?" I wasn't sure I wanted the answer to that, but I knew I needed to ask.

"No. Yes." She shook her head as she stood and began to pace. "No. I'm not afraid of you, although you can be pretty intimidating."

"I'd never hurt you."

"I know. I don't know how I know that, but I do. I've seen

evil and you're not it. It's just, well, you *could* hurt me. If you wanted to."

"Do you trust me?" I'd already asked her this once, but I'd continue to ask her until her answer was unequivocally 'yes'.

"I want to. But I've been burned by the one man I should've been able to trust above all others." The pacing stopped. Her eyelids closed, and she breathed through her nose. One breath, two… "Literally." Brie gripped the hem of her shirt and slid it up her abdomen, revealing the scars I'd seen earlier.

Careful to mask the fury that rode me, I stood up and went to her. When there were only mere inches separating our bodies, I reached out and traced a line from one scar to the next. She flinched at the first touch but relaxed by the time I got to the fifth circle that marred her otherwise flawless skin. Her breathing became choppy, and I had to force myself not to go too far, too fast.

"Your father?" I leaned in so that my heated breath washed over her.

Her mouth opened and closed several times, no words escaping. She nodded and the motion caused a tear to slip out beneath her tightly closed lids.

"I'll kill him." I was past the point of controlling my anger. My blood was boiling, and I itched to follow through on my threat. Walk out of the house and track down the fucker. Teach him a lesson he wouldn't live to remember.

Her arms came around me and she squeezed. Whether to calm herself or me, I didn't know.

"Make me forget," she mumbled into my chest.

The fury that had been building in me fled and was replaced by desire. I lifted her up, and her legs straddled my hips. My fingers threaded together to cradle her ass, and I carried her to my bedroom, kicking the door shut behind me.

When my shins hit the bed, I pulled back to examine her face. Damn, she was beautiful. Luminous eyes, full lips, long ebony hair. Her eyes lowered under my scrutiny, her earlier hesitation showing.

"Look at me." She lifted her gaze to mine, so I continued. "There's something you need to know about me."

She should know what she was asking for, begging for. Before I continued, I sat on the bed, keeping her on my lap and running my hands under her shirt and up her back.

"I've got... kinks." Her eyes widened, and she sucked in a breath. "I don't need them every time, but I think I can use them to help you."

"What kind of *kinks*?"

"I've dabbled in BDSM, but breath play is my favorite." I didn't bother mincing words.

"Breath play?"

"Yeah. While we're..." I paused and ran my fingers under her hair to gently wrap around the back of her neck, "fucking, I'd restrict the oxygen to your brain, which intensifies your pleasure." I increased the pressure, without hitting the artery necessary to do what I craved.

Brie's nostrils flared, and she leaned back into my hold. "Does it hurt?"

"Not if I do it right."

"And what happens if I decide it's too much and I want to stop?"

Silly woman. "You tap me three times and I stop. No questions asked."

She pushed against my arms, and I released her. She slid off my lap to stand. "I haven't... I just haven't. Not since him. But I wanna feel good." She ducked her head, and when she lifted it back up, she was biting her lip.

"I can make you feel so good."

Her bottom lip slipped from her teeth. "Okay."

She began to unbutton her jeans, and I stood and put my hand over hers to stop her. I wanted to unwrap this particular present.

"Let me?"

Her head bobbed up and down, and she swallowed. I reached over my shoulders to pull my shirt off, exposing my tattooed chest. Her breath hitched, and her eyes raked over my nakedness.

I got down on my knees, my eyes level with the juncture of her thighs. I tugged her zipper down and stripped the denim down her legs. Her hands came to my shoulders to steady herself. She had on black lace panties, and her curls begged to be free. I made quick work of tearing the miniscule fabric from her body.

I stood back up and gripped her hips, pulling her toward me. My hands travelled under her shirt, up her ribs, to the weight of her breasts begging to be held. Cupping her tits, I traced circles over her nipples, feeling them pebble under my touch.

When her panting increased, I stepped away and shed the rest of my clothes. I needed to feel her skin, her heat, her arousal. I reached out to tug her shirt up, and she put her hands on mine to stop them.

"Brie."

She dropped her hands to her sides and blew out a breath. I inched her shirt up and over her head, reveling in the sight of her rosy nipples straining against her black lace bra. It matched the panties that were now ruined on my floor. I flicked open the back closure with one deft hand while the other caught her left breast as it bounced free.

Her hips undulated, seeking the contact that would bring her relief. Her arousal wet my thigh, and I prayed I'd be able to last long enough to do all the things I wanted.

"Stop," I commanded.

She froze and I stepped back to admire the Venus before me. Her body shook, but otherwise, she stood still, allowing me to emblazon every sweet inch of her into my brain.

"You're beautiful." I was staring at the globes of her ass, my hands itching to be filled with her perfection.

She scoffed, but I let it go. I'd make her see what I saw. Feel what I felt.

"Turn around." She did as she was told. "This time, I'll take it easy, unless you beg for more. Do you understand?"

"Yes."

"Good. Now, lie down on the bed."

Seeing her laid out before me, mine for the taking, kicked my libido into overdrive. I leaned over her, bracing myself on my arms and effectively caging her in. Her breathing quickened, and I could see her pulse jump in her neck.

"Am I scaring you?"

"No."

"Don't lie to me." I gripped her chin and forced her eyes to mine. "Am I scaring you?"

"A little. He, uh, he used to make me feel trapped." Her tongue swept her bottom lip, leaving it glossy and begging to be sucked on.

"I'm not him." Part of me wanted to reverse our positions, but that wouldn't help her overcome her fear.

"I know."

"Do you?" I allowed my weight to settle over her, my arousal to register.

She nodded and my mouth crashed down on hers. My tongue teased the seam of her lips, probing, seeking entry. Her lips parted, and our tongues danced. It wasn't sweet or slow. It was hot and primal, both of us taking what we needed from the other.

Never ending the kiss, I lifted my hips and reached between our bodies. I took my throbbing cock in my hand

and gave it a few jerks, my knuckles scraping her clit as I did. Her moans filled the room, as did the heady scent of her excitement.

No longer able to go slow, I lined myself up at her entrance and impaled her in one quick thrust. The moaning ceased, and her eyes widened. Panic, laced with raw need, bloomed in her gaze. Her breathing sped up, and I feared she was going to pass out.

"Breathe, baby," I crooned as my movements ceased. "Just breathe."

She tried to take deeper breaths, but it didn't seem to be working.

"I'm not him. Look at me." Her eyes met mine. "I'm not him. I'm Griffin. I'm not going to hurt you."

Incapable of speech, she nodded furiously, still trying to catch her breath.

I braced myself on my elbow and used my other hand to roam her body, her face, through her hair. She slowly started to come down from her panic, and I began to rock my hips, letting my thickness ease in and out of her. She was still wet, and her walls clamped down, sucking me in further.

Balls deep, my body vibrated with pent up need. I thrust into her harder and faster, responding to the demands of her pussy. I was spiraling, and in an effort to bring her into the vortex with me, I ran my hand up over her breasts and stopped at her throat. My fingers found her pulse point and squeezed.

Her hips bucked, and her eyes went wide with panic.

"Trust me," I begged through gritted teeth. "Trust me to take care of you."

I put a little more pressure on her throat, and she milked my cock as pleasure began to replace the panic.

"That's it, baby. I've got you."

My balls began to tingle, and I knew I was close. Too

close. I quickly reversed our positions so she was straddling me, without ever taking my hand away from her neck. She looked at me with surprise.

I found her clit and rubbed fast circles over it, the rhythm matching my flying hips. She met me, thrust for thrust, as her hands clutched the one depriving her of oxygen. Just as I was about to explode, I released her throat and pulled her down, bruising her lips with my own. We swallowed each other's moans as we crashed into oblivion.

She collapsed on top of me, and I held her for several minutes before getting up and walking to the bathroom. I came back with a warm washcloth and stopped in my tracks at the sight of her sated body in my bed. Instantly, I was hard again. She peered at me and smiled.

"That was amazing." She seemed surprised.

"Of course it was." I chuckled as I sat down on the bed beside her and ran the washcloth between her thighs, cleaning up our ecstasy.

After she was clean, I tossed the washcloth onto the floor and climbed under the covers. She rolled onto her side, and I pulled her back so her ass was tucked against me. A yawn escaped her, and she wiggled to get more comfortable.

"Get some sleep." I banded my arm around her and held her tightly. After what we'd just shared, I wanted to take care of her all night long.

"G'night." Her breathing evened out and her body relaxed as she drifted off.

As I lay there, staring at the wall and feeling her lungs expand with each sleep-filled breath, I had no idea how much taking care of her, *loving her,* would consume me after that night.

11

BRIE

Present day...

Griffin had been gone for a while. When he'd left that morning, he said he had to talk to Micah but hadn't told me any specifics. Nell had taken his place as my watchdog, and while it was nice to see her, I didn't want company. Or a babysitter.

Nell had tried to talk to me, get me to open up. She'd asked me questions that I couldn't answer. She'd told me about her boyfriend, Jake, and everything I'd missed while I was *away*. I'd listened to her go on and on about things I wanted to care about but didn't.

We were sitting on the couch, and I couldn't stand it any longer. I got up and, ignoring the hurt look on her face, stalked to the kitchen. The refrigerator door banged into the wall as I yanked it open and pulled out a beer. I needed to numb the pain, the memories.

"Brie, it's only ten in the morning!" Nell exclaimed as I marched through the living room and into the bathroom.

I slammed the bathroom door and leaned against it. Nell's fists pounded, and she begged me to let her in, but I didn't listen. My own personal pharmacy was lined up on the counter and I shook out the pills and tossed them into my mouth. They sat on my tongue for a moment before I slid to the floor, took a pull of my beer and washed them down.

"Brie, open the damn door." Nell was furious. *Well, me too.* "Come on! Please!"

She gave up and her footsteps echoed as she retreated to the living room. After a few minutes, I got up and opened the door. I glanced down the hall to see Nell on her cell phone, no doubt calling in the troops. Not giving a damn, I strode to my bedroom and quietly shut the door, flipping the lock behind me.

Silence.

As I looked around my room, my eyes landed on a pile of clothes in the corner. Anger flooded my system, mixing in with the drugs and alcohol, when I zeroed in on a particular shirt. Ian had given it to me for my birthday and had gushed over the way it fit, hugging my curves while hiding my scars. He'd hated my scars.

All at once, I gripped my chest and doubled over. I couldn't breathe. I collapsed onto the floor and forced air into my lungs. I wrapped my shaking arms around my knees and rocked back and forth. Eventually, I was able to breathe again, even though the panic and anger never left me. I swiped at the tears that had fallen, and a dozen different memories assaulted my senses.

Memories of my father. Of Ian and Steve. Of *him.*

I crawled to my bed and leveraged myself up. The pocketknife on my nightstand taunted me, and I absently ran my fingers over the scars on my wrists. It wouldn't take much to finish what I'd started in that cave. I was numb enough now that I might actually be able to do it.

I sank to the floor with the pocketknife open and in my hand. I stared at it, willing it to do the hard thing for me. Emotions ricocheted through my system and sobs erupted from deep in my gut. I was helpless to stop them, but there was one thing I could do. One thing I could control.

The slice of the blade, the trickle of blood...it felt good. *So good.*

"Brie!" Griffin's voice interrupted my purge, and the door sounded like it would split open under his weight. "Brie, open the fucking door!"

My mouth opened to tell him to go away. To let me die. But nothing came out. Nothing but guttural sobs. I let the blade slice deeper and watched as the pool of blood grew bigger, thicker.

Just as I was about to pass out, the door crashed open and Griffin was next to me.

"Jesus." That one word whooshed out of him, and he grabbed the knife from me, tossing it across the room. "What have you done?"

He sounded so far away. I shivered as the blood loss did its job. Griffin yanked his shirt over his head and wrapped the material around my wrist, applying pressure.

"Nell, call Doc," Griffin yelled over his shoulder.

I had the strangest sense of déjà vu as I was lifted off the floor and cradled against his chest. Griffin sat on the bed, never letting me go. Feeling safe for the first time in what felt like forever, I let the blackness take me.

~

Muffled voices pulled me out of the thick fog encasing me, and I tried to focus on what was being said.

"Fuck, Griff. This is bad." Doc's tone reminded me of rough sandpaper. "She needs more help than we can provide."

No. No, no, no.

"Christ, Doc." Griffin's voice came from different locations in the room as he paced. A mental image surfaced of him shoving his fingers through his hair, jaw set and teeth clenched. "We're not sending her to some head shrinker."

"We may not have a choice."

Micah?

"There's always a choice," Griffin muttered. "You, more than anyone, should understand that."

"Excuse me?" Micah seethed. My gut twisted with each angry word. My circumstances were causing a rift between them.

"You heard me," Griffin snapped. "You had a choice with Sadie, but you couldn't think past your dick and look where that got us. Got Brie."

"You better watch your tone," Micah warned. "Sadie is my wife and the mother of my children, and you will not bring her into this. She's been through enough and already blames herself for what happened to Brie."

Wait. What?

Not wanting to hear them fight, I forced my eyes open, blinking several times as I adjusted to the light. I rolled to my side, drawing their attention as the sheets ruffled. Griffin was kneeling beside the bed in an instant.

He reached his hand out to caress my arm, and I pulled away from him. Hurt crossed his features, and he wrinkled his brow. He sat back on his haunches and blew a breath out.

Our gazes never wavered. He looked at me so intently, like he thought I'd disappear if he blinked. Micah walked up behind him and placed his hand on his shoulder. That's how it should be between them. Best friends. Brothers.

"Brie, how are you feeling?" Micah's tone held no trace of the anger from earlier.

I curled into a ball and brought my hands to my chest, shielding my heart. The movement made me wince when the raw wounds I'd inflicted earlier brushed against my T-shirt. Griffin's eyes narrowed in concern, and I ignored it, choosing to focus on Micah. His stare seemed to penetrate my soul, and I tried to stop the tears, but failed.

As sobs shook my body, Griffin came up to the bed and sat next to me. The mattress dipped with the addition of his weight, and I tried to scoot away from him. He wasn't having it. He pulled me back toward him, lifting my body onto his lap, cradling me.

"Shh, baby. You're safe." He rubbed circles on my back and placed gentle kisses in my hair. "Ignore them. It's just you and me."

"Brie, I'm sorry." Micah sounded devastated. Knowing him, he probably thought he was the cause of this breakdown.

I wanted to tell him it wasn't his fault. That he'd done nothing wrong. It was just...everything. But I couldn't.

The sound of retreating footsteps registered, and the sobs slowed. When I glanced around the room, no one was there. No one but the man who had chased away so many of my demons over the years. The only man who made me feel something beyond despair and simple lust.

"You should have let me die." I crawled off his lap and under the covers, turning my back on the one man who would demand more from me than I was able to give.

12

GRIFFIN

You should have let me die.

Those words have played on a loop in my head for the last four days. When Brie had made that statement and turned her back on me, I'd been stunned. She's always been strong and able to handle anything. Even on her worst day, back at boot camp, she hadn't crumbled. Not completely, anyway. Now? Now she was broken, and I worried she was beyond repair.

"VP? You with us?" Micah spoke, cutting off my thoughts.

"Huh?"

I glanced around the library at the members of the BRB. Micah had called a meeting this morning to discuss a new case. Jackson had been invited so that progress on Brie's situation could be reviewed, but he'd gone to talk to Brie first, see if she could provide any information. He had yet to arrive at the main house.

"Aiden was reporting on the new arrival in Cabin four." Micah narrowed his eyes at my lack of attention.

"Sorry," I mumbled.

"As I was saying, Tracy arrived last night. She was covered

in bruises. Tried to cover them with makeup." Aiden snorted. "Didn't work."

"Were you able to get any information from her? Full name, DOB, social? Anything on her abuser?" I asked, finally settling into the job at hand.

"Not much. Here's her wallet." He tossed the red leather on the table, and it landed with a thud in front of me. "Hopefully you can get something from it."

"I'll see what I can do." I picked up the wallet and started rifling through it. There were a few credit cards, very little cash and some tattered pictures. They appeared to be of a young woman with her parents, the resemblance strong. I held one up to Aiden. "This her?"

He grabbed the picture out of my grasp and took a closer look.

"Yeah, that's her. A little younger and a lot happier, but that's her." He sighed as he dropped the photo on top of the pile of wallet contents forming in front of me.

"It's a start. I'll try to clean the photo up a bit and run it through my facial recognition software. See if anything pops."

"Facial recognition software?" Jackson strode into the room and whistled. "Does this have anything to do with Brie?"

"Unfortunately, no," Micah responded. "New case we caught last night."

"Anything I can do?" Jackson was always ready to lend a hand.

"Not yet," I chimed in. "Aiden, give me a few days to see what I can come up with. If you get any more info that might be helpful, let me know."

"Sure thing." Done with his duty to report, Aiden plopped down in his chair and rested his forearms on the table.

"Any objections to Griffin taking a few days to dig up

information on Tracy?" Micah asked. Everyone was silent. "Good. Moving on to Brie. Jackson, why don't you fill us in on the investigation."

"Well, there's not much to tell. Brie was able to give me a name." Jackson jumped right in.

"What's his name?" I asked through gritted teeth. My hands balled into fists on the table, and my knuckles went white under the pressure.

"Now, Griffin, you know I—"

"Give me a name," I demanded, bringing my clenched fist down and rattling the glasses on the table.

"Steve. All she knows is that his first name is Steve." Jackson's shoulders rose and fell, the weight of this investigation clear.

I was out of my chair so fast, it toppled to the floor. I'd almost made it to the door before Jackson stepped in front of me.

"Get the fuck out of my way," I raged, needing to track down every Steve within a hundred-mile radius.

"Sit. Down." Micah's voice bounced off the library walls and I turned. My chest was heaving, and fire had ignited my blood. "I've given you a lot of rope lately. Don't fucking hang yourself with it."

"I've gotta find him and make him pay." I glanced around the room, seeking agreement from the others, but none came.

"And we will. Now," Micah pointed to my chair. "Sit down and shut up. Let Jackson finish."

I righted the chair and sat down with a thud.

"Please, continue." Micah waved his hand at Jackson.

"Like I said, all we have is a first name. But I'm going to go back to the station and do a search for every Steve in the county. That'll give me some photos to work with and hopefully Brie can identify him based on a picture."

"He was seen leaving the cave where she was found. How do you not know who he is yet?" Nell asked quietly. I'd forgotten she was there. She'd been so silent.

"Because he got away and my guy didn't get a good look at his face."

"And who's fucking fault is that?" I sneered.

"Griffin, we've been over this. Circumstances that were beyond our control allowed him to get away. We can't go back and change it." Jackson's face was red with anger, whether at me or his men, I had no idea. Nor did I care. "What we can do is what I just said. I'll pull together a photo lineup for Brie to go through." He took a deep breath before he continued. "If Brie could give us more information, that would be even better."

"But Brie's not talking." Doc stated the obvious.

"I'm working on it." I scrubbed my hands over my face, the last few days catching up to me. "She spoke the other day, after she tried to off herself."

All eyes snapped to me.

"What? Why didn't you say anything? What did she say?" Aiden demanded.

"Because she hasn't spoken since. And honestly, I didn't want any of you to have to live with what she said."

"What'd she say?" Nell stood and came around the table to kneel next to my chair. Her hand rested on my forearm, and I drew comfort from it.

"'You should have let me die'." My shoulders sagged. "She told me I should have let her die."

Nell's breath hitched and audible intakes of air sounded from around the room.

"I know you don't want to hear this, but have any of you considered the possibility that maybe this isn't the best place for Brie to heal?" Jackson looked around the room, meeting the eyes of everyone there but locking onto mine.

"Been there, had the conversation, got the fucking T-shirt," Micah muttered. He turned his gaze to me, and a hard look came across his face. "Griffin has assured me that he can help her heal better than anyone else, and I trust him."

He did?

"There will be no more discussion about it. This is her home. We're her family. We don't turn our back on family, no matter the circumstances." Micah let that hang in the air for a minute, practically daring anyone to contradict him.

"Jackson, how long will it take you to pull together the photos?" I turned my head to face him.

"A few days to a week."

"And if Brie can't pick this fuck out of the photo lineup, then what?"

"Then," he raised his hands, palms up, "we'll just have to keep looking."

"So, Brie's fucked. Unless she can identify him or she talks, there's no hope for justice." My indignation was bubbling over. It was never far from the surface lately, but in that moment, it couldn't be contained.

"Pretty much." Jackson shrugged and his face fell into a look of defeat.

"Griff, do you think you can get her to talk? Work your magic?" Doc looked hopeful and I hated to burst his bubble.

"I can, but it may take a while. There's so much more to her than any of you can possibly comprehend." I held my hand up to discourage their questions. "That's all you're getting from me. Micah knows everything and he trusts me. He's your president. Are you going to question his judgment?"

Heads shook and several muttered 'no's' filled the air. I stood up and cracked my knuckles.

"Good. Now, I'm going to go relieve Sadie and check in on Brie." I turned to face Aiden. "I'll grab what I need and run those checks on Tracy from her place." I pushed my chair under the table and started for the door.

"Griffin?" Micah's voice stopped me in my tracks. "Take care of our girl."

I nodded once and strode through the door, never once looking back.

13

BRIE

Something wet dripped onto my arm. I cracked one eye open and was met with the stare of Sully, Aiden's Boxer. His tongue was hanging out of the side of his mouth and a long trail of drool was falling from his jowls. I shook the slobber off my arm and swung my legs over to plant my feet on the floor.

"Sully!" Aiden's voice reached me a second before he came running through the bedroom door. He halted when he saw me awake. "Oh, sorry. He got away from me. Come, Sully." Sully went and stood at his feet. Aiden ruffled the fur on Sully's head before he looked at me again. "Griffin had to run to town. Can I get you anything?"

I shook my head. I wished everyone would quit babying me. It'd been two weeks since I'd lost my shit, and I hadn't been left alone since. Why couldn't they understand that I needed space? Time to figure myself out.

"Well." Aiden scratched his head. "I'll let you get some rest." He backed out of the room, snapping his fingers for Sully to follow.

Rest? They seriously thought I needed *more* rest. I wasn't sure what I needed, but one thing was clear. Rest was not it.

I stomped to the bathroom to take care of business, and when I was done, my stomach rumbled. I'd been eating more, re-establishing my metabolism. I'd put on a few pounds, and my face was filling out. I was finally starting to recognize my reflection in the mirror, even if I couldn't see past it to what lay beneath.

"Coffee's fresh." Aiden pointed to the coffee pot as I entered the kitchen. He pulled a mug from the cupboard and handed it to me.

I grabbed the mug from his hand and skirted around him, careful not to get too close. He watched my every movement but didn't comment.

My hands wrapped around the hot mug, letting its heat warm me. As I sat at the table, Aiden went to the stove and broke some eggs into a skillet.

"Griffin said to feed you if you came out of your room."

My eyes rolled behind his back.

"I saw that, smartass." He glanced over his shoulder and chuckled at my shocked expression. "You're forgetting the countless hours we spent together overseas. I know you can't resist a good eye roll." He punctuated that with a wink.

The reminder of who I used to be sobered me. I lowered my head and felt the tell-tale quiver of my bottom lip. I bit down so hard that I tasted blood.

"Hey, hey, hey," Aiden said as he walked toward me. He straddled the chair next to mine and turned me to face him. "Look at me."

I lifted my eyes to his, and he reached out to wipe blood from my lip. I flinched but he ignored it.

"I can't even begin to imagine how you feel, but I do know you, Brie. You're a fighter. You'll get through this." He sat there and stared at me, as if willing me to speak, to agree with him. When I didn't, he frowned before abandoning his chair and returning to the stove.

I let his words sink in. He was right, I was a fighter. Or I had been. Could I get that part of me back? I thought so but was skeptical.

How was I supposed to reconcile who I'd been with who I was now? That was the million-dollar question. It'd taken me years to move past my father's abuse, and I don't think I would have had it not been for Griffin. Add the last seven months into the mix and I was fucked.

Aiden deftly flipped the over-easy eggs, the yoke remaining intact. He turned and dropped two slices of bread into the toaster. I wanted to remind him that I liked my toast crispy, but I couldn't speak. I watched as he turned the dial on the toaster to the perfect setting and sighed at the fact that he hadn't needed reminded.

I'd never had a problem talking before. Sure, I'd had a shitty childhood but that's why I'd joined the Navy. To get away from my past and hopefully learn the skills I needed so I would never feel vulnerable again. The Navy had taught me to take no shit from anyone, and I had grown into a woman who could not only stand up for herself, but also the one who was pretty badass at protecting others.

If I was being honest with myself, Griffin had helped me too. While the Navy had given me skills and a backbone, Griffin had given me confidence. He taught me that it was okay to be scared but to push through the fear and take what I wanted. What I needed.

"Eat up," Aiden said, breaking off my thoughts. He slid a plate in front of me, but there was no fork.

I stood up and walked to the utensil drawer, pulling it out so hard that it almost came off its tracks and the silverware clattered.

"Damn. What'd that drawer ever do to you?" Aiden teased.

Part of me wanted to be mad at him, but he was actually trying. Treating me more normally than the others. In an effort to reclaim a little of my old self, I flipped him off.

"No thanks, sweetcheeks. I have a feeling that would be a good way to piss a certain someone right the fuck off."

"Who are you pissing off?" Griffin strode through the door, and his gaze swung from Aiden to me.

"No one, brother." Aiden shook his head before lowering it. I didn't miss the smile he tried to hide. "No one."

"I'm hungry. You make enough for me?" Griffin asked as he walked toward the stove.

I scurried around the table. This morning had been better than most lately, and I didn't want to ruin it.

"No. I'm not your fucking cook." Aiden muttered.

"Jesus, chill," Griffin shot back.

Their words sounded heated to my ears, and my breath caught in my throat. *I needed to get out of here.*

I picked up my plate from the table and set it on the counter, next to where Griffin was standing. He could have my food. My appetite had vanished when the panic surfaced. I looked at him, saw the confusion in his eyes, and turned and ran.

I slammed my bedroom door behind me and leaned against it. My back pressed to the wood as I slid to the floor. Several deep breaths sawed in and out of my lungs until I managed to calm myself down. Hard knocks jolted the door into my back, making the calm short-lived.

"Brie, come on. Open up," Griffin hollered through the barrier.

I shook my head before remembering he couldn't see me.

"Brie, please," he pleaded.

Unable to stand the concern in his voice, I stood and

turned to open the door. When there was no barrier between us, Griffin stepped up close, stealing my oxygen.

I clawed at my throat as I tried to suck in air.

"Breathe, baby." He said, wrapping his arms around me and forcing my hands to my sides.

I struggled against his hold, not wanting to be touched. He didn't let me go but instead, he held me tighter.

"Fight me all you want. I'm not going anywhere."

I viciously shook my head, unsure what I was saying 'no' to. His hold on me? His declaration that he wasn't going anywhere? Probably both.

His hands worked their way up my back until he had one hand gripped around the nape of my neck. The warmth of his fingers and the pressure he was initiating had me calming. *Yes.* He knew what I needed, and I thanked God he didn't need me to tell him.

"Is this what you want?" He always asked, and I knew he was able to read all my cues so there was no fear.

I nodded, tears streaming down my face.

"Breathe, baby." He increased the pressure. "Close your eyes and trust me."

His voice washed over me, and I relished what I knew was coming. His fingers gradually compressed my throat and euphoria seeped in. It was ironic that he told me to breathe when he was stealing my breath. That was my last thought before everything around me fell away and I was flying.

14

GRIFFIN

I scooped Brie's limp form into my arms and carried her to the bed. Her breathing was calm, and her face was relaxed. I allowed myself several minutes to watch her sleep. I'd put off facing Aiden for as long as I could.

"She okay?"

I whipped around to see him standing in the doorway with his hands in his pockets.

"She is now," I whispered, walking toward him.

I closed the door behind me and winced as the latch clicked. I listened for any sound coming from inside. When there was none, I released the breath I'd been holding.

"What spooked her?" Aiden sat on the couch once we reached the living room. "She seemed to be okay and then, bam." He shook his head in a show of frustration.

"She's not okay," I said through clenched teeth.

"I get that, but it was like, I don't know, man. There was a little more light in her eyes."

"Don't worry about it. I've got it covered."

He didn't push, likely sensing I didn't want to talk about

it. I'd already broken Brie's trust once. I wasn't going to do it again.

"So, uh, I've been digging into Tracy." I scratched my head, trying to figure out where to even start.

"Yeah? Get anything?"

"You're not gonna like it." I walked to the desk I'd been working at while staying with Brie and picked up the stack of papers outlining all that I'd found. "For starters, there's this." I tossed the first few pages onto his lap.

Aiden picked them up and his eyebrows rose as he read the letterhead on the top page. *Massachusetts Institution for the Criminally Insane.*

"Seriously?" He glanced at me but didn't wait for an answer before he skimmed the rest of the information.

"Seems she's pretty well known there. They've reported her missing." I showed him the missing person report. It included a photo of Tracy, but without the bruises she had when she'd arrived.

"What the hell? Her face had been black and blue when she got here." He glanced up at me. "Think she did it to herself?"

"Kinda seems that way. I think you need to get Jackson out here and let him handle it."

"Yeah. Yeah, okay." He shoved his hands through his hair. This had to be hard for him. He was usually a good judge of character, but he'd missed this. "I'm gonna get on that." He had his phone to his ear, barking orders at whatever poor fool answered to *find Jackson now,* before he'd even walked out the door.

I sat down at the desk and opened my laptop to do a little research of my own. I'd been combing through every database I could think of since Brie had given us the name Steve. Jackson had been right. Without any leads, this was no easy task. But that didn't mean I would stop trying.

As I sifted through image after image on the screen, I lost track of time. Social media was where I was currently hunting, but it was a black hole of information. Maybe I was going about this all wrong, searching for the wrong person. With that in mind, I pulled up my facial recognition software and ran a search for Brie. I hated the thought that some sick fuck would post pictures of her, but I'd try anything at this point.

I'd gotten through five websites, and just when I was about to give up, my software stopped and emitted a loud beep, indicating it'd found a match. I zeroed in on the screen, and my gut twisted. Right in front of me, in full color, was a picture of Brie, naked on the floor of the cave. She appeared unconscious and was covered in blood, dirt and bruises.

I picked up my phone and dialed Jackson, needing him to see this. The call went to voicemail. Rather than leave a message, I copied the link to the photo and emailed it to him. Then I sent him a quick text.

Me: Check your email and call me!

Everything in me screamed *find him*. Good ol' Steve hadn't been stupid enough to post the picture under his own name, but I could trace it back to him. It would just take some time. Before I could do any of that, I needed a break to clear my head. I was hungry, and I wanted to check on Brie. I stood and stretched my arms above my head, popping my neck to ease the tension.

My stomach growled as I walked to the kitchen to make a couple of sandwiches. Brie hadn't eaten breakfast, and I needed to make sure she ate lunch. I set the food-laden plates on the table and started toward Brie's room. As I stepped into the living room, I froze.

Brie stared at the image on my laptop, her hand covering

her mouth. I stormed to the desk and slammed the laptop closed. I slowly turned around, dreading what I'd see. Brie hadn't moved. Her molten eyes were wide and the hand in front of her face shook. She stood there, unmoving, tears snaking down her cheeks.

"Brie, baby. I'm sorry." There was nothing else I could say.

She whirled around to run, and my hand snaked out to stop her. I gripped her arm and forced her to face me. She exuded pain, and all I wanted to do was take it away. And kill the motherfucker that'd caused it.

That's you, asshole.

Brie struggled against my hold, but she was no match for me. I wrapped my arms around her and rested my chin on her head. In a moment of weakness, all I felt was her curves and the way she fit perfectly tucked against me. Her trembling no longer registered. I breathed in her scent, giving in to the moment.

Brie shoved out of my hold and took two steps back. Her gaze traveled from my face, down my body, stopping at the straining bulge that had caused her to push away. Questions danced in her eyes as they darted to my face.

"I can't help it." I sighed and adjusted myself in an effort to stop scaring her. "You've had this effect on me since the moment I saw you."

She shook her head from side to side, denying what I'd said. Her feet carried her away from me. For every step she took back, I took one toward her.

"You can't run from this. From me."

When I was close enough to touch her, I reached my hand out. She slapped it away.

"Feel better?" I taunted. I reached out again, and before she could slap me away, I gripped her tiny hand in my much larger fist, stopping her assault.

Her eyes blazed as she tried to pull away. Her efforts were

useless. I wasn't going to hurt her, and she knew it. I just had to prove it to her...again.

"Do you remember that night at the Quarterdeck?" I asked, tipping my head to the picture of us on the wall.

She looked toward the picture and nodded.

"Were you afraid of me that night?"

Again, she nodded. Her brows crinkled and her confusion at my point registered.

"Did I hurt you?"

I locked eyes with her and willed her to answer. She lowered her gaze under the intensity of my stare and my dick sprang to life.

"Brie, look at me."

She raised her head and gave me a challenging stare.

"Did I hurt you?"

She stood there for a minute, still not answering. After a few deep breaths, she shook her head.

"Do you trust me?"

Brie nodded, albeit slowly.

"Are you afraid of me right now?"

Again, her gaze lowered to the floor and she shrugged.

"I would never hurt you. You have to know that." Unable to stop myself, I said, "I love you too much."

Her head snapped to mine, and distress infused her stare. Her feet carried her backward until she ran into the wall.

"Brie—"

She shook her head wildly before she turned and fled to her room. I let her go because really, what could I say?

15

BRIE

Life was a cruel bitch.

The room was spinning, and I couldn't make it stop. When I'd seen that picture of me, I'd immediately been transported back in time. Living through that hell had been bad enough, but now there were pictures of it out there for the world to see. For men to get their jollies off on my pain and suffering.

I sat down on the bed and stared at the wall, willing the tilt-a-whirl I was on to stop. I wanted off. Eventually, the room came back into focus, and when it did, the floodgates of my mind opened.

As if my life weren't fucked enough, I had to face the fact that Griffin loved me? Where the hell had that come from? I'd loved Griffin Strong for ten years and *now* he decides to love me back. Now, when I'm incapable of life, let alone love.

I had to get the fuck out of here. Griffin thought he could love me back to my old self, but that wasn't possible. No way in hell could I stick around and hurt him. Because that's exactly what would happen if I stayed. He'd keep trying to fix me and love me, and I'd keep pushing him away.

I wanted to get better. I really did. I just didn't know how to make that happen. Being here, where my world crashed and burned, was not the place to start. Maybe if I could get away I could start to find myself again.

The floorboards creaked outside my bedroom door, and I held my breath, hoping he couldn't hear me.

Hear what? You can't talk!

"Brie, I'm sorry. I shouldn't have said that."

Ya think?

"I know you're scared and you think you don't deserve love."

How the hell did he know that?

"But you do. God, you deserve the world. I want to be the man to give it to you."

No! Stop! Why now?

"Baby, please."

I can't!

I heard him sigh, sounding almost as broken as I felt.

"Fine. I'll leave you alone for now, but this doesn't change anything. I love you, and I'll be here when you're ready to talk."

Talk? I can't fucking talk, asshole!

His footsteps retreated, and I prayed he'd leave the house entirely. He didn't. Instead, I heard the steady thrumming of his fingers flying across his keyboard. *More research?*

I stretched out on the bed, my arms underneath my head. I had a plan to formulate. I couldn't stay here. That was crystal clear. Everyone in the BRB was doing everything they could to help, but they were suffocating me. As I contemplated how I could leave without getting stopped by anyone, my eyelids grew heavy.

Please, God, let them have kept up with Chaos's maintenance while I was gone.

That was my last thought before I surrendered to sleep.

My eyes opened and I registered the shift in the shadows dancing around my room. I glanced toward the window. It was evening and the sun was setting.

I swung my legs over the bed and paused as I strained to hear if there was movement in the cabin. Silence greeted me. I crept to the window and drew back the sheer curtain, trying to get a glimpse of the driveway.

Perfect. Amina was gone, which meant Griffin was too. I rushed to my closet and grabbed my go-bag. The contents of the bag were burned in my brain, so there was no reason to check and see if it held everything I would need. It did. Almost.

My gun was heavy in my hand as I snatched it from my nightstand. I ignored the foreign sensation and shoved it in the bag. Satisfied that I had everything, I went to the kitchen to grab a few bottles of water and protein bars. There wasn't much room for anything more than that in my saddlebags. I'd stop for real food once I was miles away.

When I reached the front door, I paused, hand on the knob. I turned around and glanced around the cabin that had been my home for several years. Memories assaulted me, and guilt infused my system.

As tears silently ran down my cheeks, I walked to the desk and picked up a pen and paper. No matter how scared I was, Griffin deserved better than me walking out without a word. He was the one constant in my life, and the least I could do was make an attempt to say good-bye.

After several false starts, the words flowed. When I got to the end, I bit my lip and agonized over how to sign it.

~~From, Brie~~
~~See you later, Brie~~
~~Sorry, The girl who is too broken~~

~~Sincerely, Me~~
I settled on...
Love, Brie

I dropped the letter on the coffee table. Without a backward glance, I strode out the door and made my way to the garage.

Chaos sat there, begging to be ridden. I threw my stuff into the saddlebags and straddled my old friend. A smile bloomed, and for the first time, I thought there might be a light at the end of this very dark tunnel.

Chaos carried me out of the garage and down my meager driveway. I nervously watched my surroundings as I drove off BRB property, praying that no one came after me. I'd driven sixty miles before my nerves settled and I felt sure that I'd gotten away unnoticed.

When I left, I hadn't been sure where I was going, but the longer I drove, the clearer my destination became. I was headed back to where my story started.

I was headed to the Bronx.

16

GRIFFIN

"Get the fuck off me!"

"Not gonna happen, babe."

My arms were full of thrashing female, and I dodged her head when she snapped it back.

"They're the ones that need to be locked up! Not me!"

"Tell that to the judge," Jackson muttered as he sifted through the paperwork Aiden had provided him.

Aiden had called me shortly after Brie dozed off. He and Jackson had been having a hard time with Tracy and needed backup. I hadn't wanted to leave Brie, but I knew I needed to talk to Jackson anyway. I'd managed to trace the photo back to Steve and finally had a last name.

When I arrived at cabin four, Tracy had been sticking to her story about being an abuse victim, but that changed once we started showing her the evidence we'd gathered. Jackson had managed to get her cuffed, and we followed them to the station so Jackson could take statements as to Tracy's mental state when she had arrived at the BRB.

The ride on Amina did wonders to clear my head. I was still berating myself for saying those all-important words to

Brie, but I couldn't take them back now. More importantly, did I even want to take them back?

No.

I meant them and refused to feel any guilt for that.

"You're hurting me." Tracy's tone was whiny and went through me like fork tines scraping on a plate.

"Suck it up, buttercup." Aiden no longer had any sympathy for the woman. He chuckled at the spectacle of me struggling to keep her in line, and my impatience rose.

"Jackson? Care to speed this shit up?" I had better things to do than man-handle this chick. Like talk to him about what I'd found.

"Sit her ass down." He pointed to the chair in the corner of the room, and I dragged Tracy over and forced her to sit. She immediately tried to stand, so I shoved her back down.

"Stay." She must have heard the fury that was threatening to boil over because she obeyed.

"This is police brutality, and I'll have your jobs," she hissed.

Aiden came to stand next to me and mimicked my pose. Arms crossed over his chest and feet braced apart, he stared down at the woman he'd grossly misjudged. Tension rolled off of him in waves.

"Sweetheart, with your history, you'll be lucky to see the outside of a padded cell. Forget ruining our jobs. Your world is about to be turned upside down."

I watched in horror as spit flew from Tracy's mouth, hitting Aiden square in the face. His eyes widened with shock, and he scrubbed the fluid off his cheek with the back of his hand.

"Do that again and see what happens," he said through clenched teeth.

"Aw, did the big bad biker man get his feelings hurt?" She slumped back in the chair and crossed her arms under her breasts. Had she not been so crazy, I might have admired the way her cleavage spilled over the low-cut top. But she was fucking certifiable. Literally.

"Lady, shut up," Jackson said.

"That's it." I turned to Jackson who was still reading through papers. "Jackson, I'm outta here." I couldn't stick around and watch this bitch tear down my brother and not do anything about it. "Call me when you're done. We need to talk about the other… investigation." Jackson's eyes lit up at that, but he didn't take it any farther. He wouldn't discuss Brie's case in front of a stranger.

"Aiden." I stopped at the doorway and turned to face him.

"Yeah?"

"Good luck."

"Thanks, asshole," he chuckled and flipped me the bird.

Heads turned as I walked through the station, but I ignored the stares and stormed out the door and down the steps. The sun had set, and anticipation settled in my gut. This was my favorite time to take Amina out. Other than the roar of my bike, there were minimal sounds to distract from the beauty and solitude of a ride through the country.

When I straddled Amina and let her vibration rush through me, I realized that the anticipation I felt was not just for a soothing ride. I was anxious to get home to Brie and make sure she was okay. The dark still scared her, and I'd been gone much longer than I'd planned.

I made the ride through town slower than usual. The streets were quiet and there was little traffic. When I reached the town limits, I let Amina's power take over and flew down the highway. I'd counted four other cops, besides Jackson, at the station, so I knew none would be out to catch me speeding.

When I reached the edge of BRB property, my phone

vibrated against my thigh. I slowed Amina and pulled off to the side of the road to answer it.

"Yeah?" I didn't want to talk to anyone. I just wanted to see Brie.

"Griffin, it's Jackson. Where the hell did you find that picture?"

"Some website dedicated to some fucked up shit." I said through clenched teeth.

"Shit." Jackson's sigh came through the line. "Were you able to trace it back to Steve?"

"Of course." I scoffed. "Holcomb. Steve Holcomb. That's our guy."

"I'll start seeing what we can find on—"

"Already did. Sent everything to your inbox."

I heard the sound of a keyboard in the background. "Got it. I'll do some more digging and take it from here."

"You're not keeping me out of this." I thrust my free hand through my hair. "I can do things on the right side of the law if you keep me informed, or I can do things the way I'd really like to do them. Track him down myself and send him straight to hell. Either way, I'm a part of his downfall."

"We'll see," Jackson said before the line went silent.

I shoved my phone back in my pocket, anger flowing through me. I'd already been a mess after the scene at the police station, and now my blood was boiling. I wanted to be in control of my emotions before allowing myself to be anywhere near Brie.

Deep breaths helped to cool my system, and I was able to ride the rest of the way home after several minutes. When I passed the main house, loud music blared, and I shook my head thinking about the younger members partying. They didn't do it often, as we weren't that kind of club, but they were young. And dumb. I'd been young and dumb once, too. I passed Micah's house, the porch light illuminating the structure. Shadows danced behind the curtains, and a pang of jealousy shot through me when I thought of him in there with his little family.

The closer I got to Brie's cabin, on the other side of the property, the more anxious I felt. Something wasn't right. No lights were on, which was odd for someone who was afraid of the dark. I told myself that she was just still sleeping, but when I pulled into the driveway, I knew I was wrong.

Her garage door was open, and Chaos was gone.

I jumped off Amina and ran to the cabin. I took the steps two at a time and barreled through the front door.

"Brie!" I already knew there wouldn't be an answer, but I yelled anyway.

I stomped through the cabin, my heart threatening to beat out of my chest. Darkness greeted me everywhere I looked. In her bedroom, I pulled open her closet door and swore viciously at the absence of her go-bag.

Fuck!

Terror washed over me. I'd never even considered that she might leave, and with her suicide attempts, my world spun on its axis. I pulled out my cell phone and speed-dialed Micah as I walked back to the living room and flipped the light on.

"This better be important," Micah answered on the third ring.

"Brie's gone." I didn't bother with pleasantries.

"What do you mean, 'Brie's gone'?"

"What do you think it means? She split." I shoved my free hand through my hair as I paced the room. The walls were closing in around me. "Her go bag is missing, and Chaos is gone."

"Be there in five." The line went dead.

Patience was not a virtue I possessed at that moment, but I forced myself to sit down on the couch and wait. As I did, a piece of paper on the coffee table caught my attention. Brie's handwriting jumped out at me when I picked it up, and my breath hitched. The paper was stained with dried tears, and I hesitated to read the words, apprehension that it would be a suicide note taking over. I forced air into my lungs and braced myself for the worst.

Griffin-

I don't even know where to start. I was going to just leave, but you deserve better from me. You've been the best friend anyone could ask for and you've helped me through so much. Back at boot camp, I was lost. You helped me find my way and brought out the best of me. For years, I loved you but the timing was never right. We couldn't be together when we were in the military and when we got out, you left.

The paper crumpled in my fist. I didn't want to read on. What she said was true. I had left. We all had. But if I'd known she loved me, I'd have stayed. *Right?* Why the fuck hadn't she told me? Needing to read the rest, I smoothed out the paper on my jean-clad knee and continued.

When Micah brought us all back together, I thought that maybe there would be a chance for us. But it wasn't meant to be. I decided that I needed to move on, and that's exactly what I did. Moved on to a monster that would make it impossible for me to love myself, let alone anyone else.

I don't know where I'll go, but I can't stay. You say you love me, but how could you? I'm damaged. Broken. Unlovable. I can't give you what you want. What you deserve. So I'm taking myself out of the equation. I want you to move on and find a woman who can give you everything. One who can love you back and not shrink in fear when you walk into a room.

Please don't try to find me. I know how you work and you

know I'll do everything I can to keep myself hidden. Don't waste your time. I'm not worth it.

Tell the others I said goodbye. Give them all a hug for me. Tell them...tell them I'm sorry.

Because I am. So sorry.

I will never forget what you've done for me over the years.

Please, let me go. I want to remember you with a smile on your face.

~~From, Brie~~
~~See you later, Brie~~
~~Sorry, The girl who is too broken~~
~~Sincerely, Me~~
Love, Brie

As I finished the letter, I pictured Brie standing at her desk, agonizing to find the right words. I was floored at her admission that she'd loved me. As I skimmed the letter a second time, the front door to the cabin flew open and slammed against the wall. Footsteps thudded against the hardwood behind me, but I didn't move. I knew who it was.

"Where'd she go?"

"I don't know, Mic."

The couch dipped when Micah sat. He snatched the letter from my hand, and I didn't fight him on it. I was too emotionally spent to care what he read. His mouth moved as he skimmed the words and every so often, his eyes would cut to mine.

"Jesus Christ." The letter drifted to the table as he released it from his grasp.

He fished his cell phone out of his pocket and punched in a number.

"Aiden, it's Micah," he said into the device. "Get over to Griff's place. Now!"

Micah's head bobbed up and down as he listened to the other side of the conversation.

Unable to sit there any longer, I stood and stalked to the kitchen. I snagged a beer from the fridge, twisted the cap off and flipped it onto the counter. As I finished a long pull from the longneck, Micah came into the room.

"You okay?"

"Fuck, no, I'm not okay." I slammed the bottle onto the counter, wincing when it shattered and sliced into my palm.

Micah didn't say a word as he went to the cupboard above the sink and pulled down the bottle of Jack Daniels Brie kept. He grabbed a highball glass off the shelf on the opposite wall and filled it with the amber liquid.

"Drink this." He shoved the glass under my nose. I downed the entire contents in one long gulp and held it out for a refill. He obliged and I downed that. The Jack burned a path to my gut and did nothing to ease my tense state.

I held the glass out again and Micah ignored me, putting the bottle back in the cupboard. I walked toward the sink and Micah's arm shot out to stop me.

"No more."

"Fuck off," I seethed.

"The others are on their way. I don't need you sloppy drunk right now. Let's go over this with everyone, and if you want to drink yourself into oblivion after that, be my guest."

I yanked a chair out from under the table and sat. He was right. I needed to keep my wits about me so we could plan. Then I'd drink until I couldn't form a coherent thought or feel a damn thing.

"They're here." The sound of motorcycles punctuated his statement, and I let it wash over me.

"What's going on?" Doc yelled from the front of the cabin. He'd been the first one in, but the others quickly followed, practically tripping over each other to get into the kitchen.

"Brie took off." My words were hollow, devoid of all emotion.

"Why are we just sitting here? We need to go find her." Nell's voice rose an octave.

I stood and walked to the living room to grab the letter. I briefly thought about grabbing my laptop to show them what I'd found, but decided against it. No need to embarrass Brie. Jackson had the photo, and the bastards name, and that's what mattered.

When I walked back into the kitchen, I handed it over to Nell and sat back down. I remained silent as everyone took turns reading it, past the point of giving a damn if anyone knew how I felt.

"Wait," Aiden said, halfway through his turn reading. "You told her you love her?"

"Yep. You got a problem with that?" My eyes bore into his, daring him to question my feelings.

"No problem. Just—"

My chair tipped over when I stood and got in his face.

"Just what? I'm not good enough for her? She deserves better? What?"

"Griffin!" Micah snapped from behind me.

"No, pres. I wanna hear this." I never looked away from Aiden. "What the fuck is it you want to say to me, Aiden?"

"All I was going to say, you crazy bastard, is it's about damn time."

"What?" My body deflated as all of my indignation left me.

"You're the only one who thinks you're not good enough. You don't think we could see how you felt about her?" He shook his head. "Shit. You should see the way you look at her when she walks into a room. And forget how you were when she was missing. You were a walking shell of the man you used to be, and when we found her? You became a regular old mama bear."

"He's right," Nell broke in. "We could all see it. We were just wondering if you even had a clue."

A new thought caused my anger to surge.

"Did any of you know?" I scanned the room, letting my gaze momentarily stop on each person in the room.

"Know what?" Doc asked.

"That she loved me."

There were muffled 'no's' and shaking heads. I released the breath I'd been holding. As I righted my chair, Micah spoke up.

"We need to figure out where she went. I'm inclined to leave her be for a while. Respect her wishes. But I'll be damned if we sit back and don't at least confirm her location and that she's safe."

"I second that," Nell said.

"Shall we put it to a vote?" Micah asked.

Everyone nodded.

"All in favor of finding her but respecting her space, raise your hand."

The only hand that didn't go up was mine.

"Griff, what do you want to do?" Aiden asked.

"I'm not fucking leaving her alone! I have half a mind to take her over my knee and spank some sense into her," I growled.

"You won't get her back that way," Nell said softly.

"Goddammit!" My fist went through the wall, and pain exploded in my knuckles. "Fine. We'll do it your way."

"It's not forever, Griff. We just need to give her some time." Nell's hand touched my shoulder, and I shrugged it off.

"I'm leaving in the morning to find her. Once I do, she has one month. One month to figure shit out. After that, all bets are off. Now," I turned away from the wall to face them, "get the fuck out of here."

No one challenged me, and there were several back slaps

as the men walked out. Nell didn't leave with the others. My eyebrows rose as I glared at her.

Her arms came around my waist and she squeezed. I hugged her back, giving her as much comfort as I was taking.

"We'll get her back, Griff."

"I know."

She released me and walked toward the front door. Before she crossed the threshold, she looked over her shoulder.

"Love ya, asshole."

"Love you too, Half-pint."

When I was finally alone, I pulled out the bottle of Jack and didn't bother with a glass. I sat on the couch and drank myself into the darkness.

17

BRIE

Metallica's "Enter Sandman" pulled me from my nightmare-filled sleep. I reached over and slapped the radio alarm clock to ease the pounding it caused. The smell of stale cigarettes wafted off the scratchy blanket the motel provided in their guestrooms. I'd been here for a week and still couldn't get used to the filth.

As I padded to the bathroom, I ignored the way my feet stuck to the stained carpet with each step. I flipped the fluorescent light on and caught my reflection in the mirror. The bags under my eyes and the gray pallor of my skin only served to remind me that I hadn't slept more than two hours a night since leaving Indiana. I'd wake up drenched in sweat and stinking of fear.

I sighed in disgust before cranking on the hot water from the shower, slipping out of my bikini briefs and T-shirt and stepping under the meager spray. As the water sluiced over my body, I mentally prepared myself for the day.

It was my birthday, and I was going to spend it in prison. As a visitor, sure, but considering who I was visiting, the prison extended beyond the boundaries of the penitentiary and invaded my soul. Just thinking about it caused my chest to constrict. Tentacles wrapped around me, stealing my breath.

Waves of panic washed over me and my mind raced to find ways to alleviate the sensation. *Griffin.* He was the one person who could help, but he wasn't here. And I'd never see him again, so I needed to figure this out. I tried to picture the ways Griffin would ease my pain and wondered if I could mimic anything he did.

As that thought took hold, my fingers trailed over my nipples, pinching and twisting in an effort to induce pleasure. It wasn't perfect but the panic lessened. Visions of Griffin hovering over me, hands wrapped around my throat floated through my mind and I craved them. One hand remained to tweak my nipple while the other trailed over the scars on my stomach, down to the heat my mind created.

My legs shook as my finger circled my clit and then dipped in between swollen lips to gather the slick moisture that mixed with the water. The hysteria I'd been feeling morphed into something else entirely as my history with Griffin fueled my ministrations. My finger returned to my clit, and I increased the pressure and speed. I became crazed in my efforts, as if climaxing would allow me to purge the demons that had ridden me for so long.

As I grew closer to release, I inserted two fingers into my pussy and continued the assault on my clit with my thumb. Within seconds of that combination, my walls contracted, and a guttural groan tore out of me.

Happy fucking birthday.

The second the high wore off, disgust surged through my system. My knees buckled, and I collapsed on the tub floor. I was grateful the panic was gone, but nothing had changed. I wasn't healed. The villains in my story remained.

This is why you're here. To slay the proverbial dragons.

I forced myself to stand and wash my hair. When I was done, I ignored the dingy towel and opted to air dry. The blinds in the room were drawn, and no one would see me. I spent the next several minutes searching for my cell phone before I remembered that I'd traded it in for a flip phone with a new number. I couldn't be without some sort of way to communicate, should it be necessary, but I wanted to reduce the chances of the BRB tracking me.

I finger-combed my hair, then threw on jeans and a black long-sleeved tee. On my way out the door, I grabbed the worn bomber jacket I'd picked up at the local thrift store. I breathed a sigh of relief when I spotted Chaos. It was always a crapshoot if he'd still be here every morning, but I'd had no other options.

I'd tried to take him in the room the first night, but the manager had raged at me and threatened to call the cops. That would only end in the BRB tracking me down, so I took my chances. I would have tried to take him inside again, but the prick from night one was always giving me disapproving glances out of the streaked window. My aim was to be as invisible as possible, not invite attention.

The drive to the prison was a long one, and it gave me time to compose my thoughts before facing off with the jackass who'd raised me. Over the last week, I've been forced to use my voice. Meals didn't order themselves in restaurants, after all. Little by little, speaking became less awkward, and I was hoping that progress wouldn't fail me today. Granted, I hadn't had a full conversation with anyone, but I'd said more words in the last seven days than I had in the last eight months.

Images of my father blended with the scenery as I sped along the New York highways. He'd been drunk the last time I'd seen him. Drunk and mean. My hand subconsciously sought out my stomach as I thought of the many times he'd burned me. The creepy smile that would form as he took his pleasure and the grunts that he would emit were memories that I wanted to forget but couldn't. Not on my own anyway.

I forced the images away and focused on what I would say to him, if anything at all.

Would he know what today was? I doubted it, and really, did it matter?

No.

He didn't matter. Did he?

Yes.

I needed to face him, face my past, before I could overcome my present and maybe have a future.

The prison gates came into view, and I slowed Chaos to pull off to the side of the road. After I stopped, I reached into my saddlebags to pull out my I.D., knowing it was required to gain entry. Before proceeding to the gate, I took one last mental inventory.

Was I ready for this?

No.

Was I going to do it anyway?

Fuck yes.

The guard that checked my I.D. flicked his gaze back and forth between me and the photo, his eyebrows arching in question. I looked nothing like the woman in the picture, so his skepticism didn't surprise me.

"Who're you here to see?" He handed the plastic card back to me and I shoved it into my back pocket.

"Uh…"

"You okay?" He looked at me like I had a screw loose. Probably seemed so with the way I kept opening and closing my mouth like a fish gasping for breath.

Sweat beaded on my forehead, and the air became too thick for my lungs.

"Look, lady, I need to know who you're here to see. Either

answer or turn around and let me get to the others." He pointed to the line of cars that had started to form behind me.

"Uh, I'm here..." I took a deep breath and peered at him as he waited. "Coleman. Ron Coleman." The words sounded more like a question than an answer.

"Coleman? You sure?"

"Yes." *No.*

"Okay, then." He shrugged his large shoulders, causing his bullet-proof vest to shift. There was a time when I'd have allowed myself to appreciate the man for what he was. Total eye-candy. That was a long time ago, though. Now I just wanted him to let me through so I could get this over with. "Are you scheduled for a visit?"

Shit. Did I have to be?

"No, I um, came from out of state. It's my birthday." I hoped he'd take pity on me and overlook the fact that I was ill-prepared.

He picked up a red phone and I listened as he spoke to someone about an 'unscheduled visit'. When he was done, he dropped the phone back in its cradle and returned his attention to me.

"Go on ahead. You'll have to sign in, and someone will be out to get you when there's a free room."

"Oh, um, okay. Thanks." I throttled Chaos and drove over the winding road that led to the disturbingly impressive fortress that housed my father.

Once inside, I sat on one of the hard plastic chairs that were reserved for the family and friends of the incarcerated. For people like me. After an indeterminate amount of time, I heard my name over a loudspeaker. I stood and walked toward a steel door that opened as I approached. On the other side was a guard who walked me toward a room encased in glass.

"Have a seat. He'll be in shortly."

I did as instructed, taking in the details of the cold room. There were two chairs, one on either side of a metal table. The top of the table had an iron hook, presumably to secure the inmate's handcuffs. There was an identical hook on the floor under the table, for leg restraints. *Surely I'd be safe here.* The glass I'd noticed when I entered appeared to be a mirror, but experience with our work in the BRB had taught me it was two-way glass. Someone would be watching this entire visit. Fine by me. It was an extra layer of security, and it helped to settle my nerves. Not enough to stop my bouncing leg or tapping fingers, but I didn't think much would stop that.

"Princess."

I was wrong. That one word stopped my movements. My entire body went rigid at the nickname that used to make me feel special. Until he'd turned it into one that made me feel...dirty. Used. Broken.

"Ron." I turned toward the man standing just inside the door. He was wearing an orange jumpsuit and was flanked by two armed guards.

"Have a seat, Coleman." Both guards had a firm grip on my father's arms and led him to the chair, shoving him down into it before securing his shackles to the iron hooks. His escorts retreated to opposite corners, remaining in the room with us.

Even better.

"What're you doing here?" Ron tilted his head as he studied me.

"I have no idea," I muttered, lowering my head.

"What?"

"Nothing." I squared my shoulders and lifted my gaze to his face.

We sat there in silence for several minutes, staring at one

another. His face was different than I remembered. It was pudgy and covered by graying stubble. There was a scar above his right eyebrow that hadn't been there, along with the one I'd given him on his left cheek the last time I'd seen him.

"As much as I'm intrigued by this little...visit," he sneered, "I'd just as soon go back to my cell than face your judgment. Why are you here?"

"Why'd you do it?" The question tore out of me before I could think it through.

"Do what, princess?" The creepy smile I remembered so well appeared, and fury replaced my nerves.

"Don't call me that," I snapped. "You lost that right the first time you touched me." I didn't give a damn if the other two in the room heard. They already knew why he was here.

"So that's what this is. You want an apology or something?" He relaxed into the chair, as much as the restraints would let him. His bored demeanor sent fury ricocheting through my system.

"You giving one?"

"No. Nothing to apologize for."

I snorted and my gaze darted to the guard I could see. How did they put up with this depravity on a daily basis and not lose their minds? The BRB came to the forefront of my thoughts, and suddenly, I understood how. They were here to serve and protect, not judge. That wasn't their purpose. Didn't make it suck any less.

"You destroyed my childhood. Broke my innocence. Broke *me*."

"You seem to be doing pretty well for yourself. No worse for the wear." He tried to wave his hand in a flippant gesture, but the cuffs halted his movement.

"Fuck you," I said through gritted teeth. "I'm a shell of the person I became after I left."

"You mean after you attacked me and got me locked up!" He was yelling, and the guards stepped closer to him.

"You attacked me!" I came out of my chair and slammed the palms of my hands on the table. "Over and over, night after night."

"I took what was mine." He said it so simply. Like it was normal to do what he did.

"Do you even realize how fucked up that sounds? I was your *child*. A little girl who didn't have a choice but to rely on you. Well, guess what?"

I glared at him and let that question hang in the air. He just glared back with a smug smile.

"I'm a big girl now, and I refuse to give you space in my thoughts for one more single second. You're not worth the air you breathe and certainly not mine."

My footsteps echoed as I walked to the door. As I waited for the door to open, his words made me cringe.

"Happy birthday, princess."

The door opened, and I rushed down the sterile hallway toward the exit. I didn't slow until I reached Chaos, but before climbing on, every emotion, every fear, came spewing out of me. I heaved until there was no more bile left to expel.

I swiped my mouth with the back of my hand, straddled Chaos, and sped away from my past. It was time to reclaim my present.

18

GRIFFIN

The sound of her retching reached my ears through the open window, and my gut twisted. I wanted to go to her, wrap her in my arms and tell her everything would be okay. I couldn't do that, though. I'd given my word to the BRB that I would give her one month, and I was nothing if not loyal.

I'd tracked Brie down after three days. She'd tried to disappear, and if I were being honest, she'd done a pretty damn good job. But I'd done better. It didn't hurt that everyone had a price, and I'd forked over my fair share of cash to get people to talk.

As Brie took off out of the prison parking lot, I waited. The air in the rental car was stale, and I missed Amina. I'd known the roar of my bike would give me away, so I'd left her at home. Part of me wished I had her so Brie would notice me tailing her. It would end the wait of the next twenty-three days, and I wouldn't be breaking a promise.

After five minutes, I started the engine and headed toward the ramshackle motel Brie had chosen. Once there, I strolled into my room, three doors down from Brie. I dropped to the bed, tugging my phone out of my pocket as I did.

"Yeah?" Micah answered on the fifth ring. Babies cried in the background, and Micah mumbled something I wasn't able to make out.

"Bad time?" I asked.

"Yeah, but it's all good. Isabelle's hungry and Sadie's feeding Isaiah, so she's making her impatience known."

"I'll keep it short. She went to the prison today. Visited her father." A sigh tore out of me, frustration laced with desperation. "I should've been with her."

"Maybe so, but she chose to do it alone. She's a big girl, Griff. You've gotta trust her."

"Yeah, yeah. Don't have to like it."

"True." There was a muffled sound, like he covered the phone with his hand. "Listen, I gotta go. Call me tomorrow."

The line went dead and I tossed my phone on the bed beside me. Now what? I couldn't sit in this shitty room all day, but I didn't want to risk being seen either.

I stood and walked to the table where my laptop was. Might as well do a little work. Brie had surprised me when she'd gone to the prison, and I didn't like surprises. Where would she go next?

It didn't take me long to realize that there wasn't anywhere else. I knew she wouldn't go to her childhood home. There was nothing left there for her. Who am I kidding? I'd never dreamed she'd go see her father, so I really couldn't say with any degree of certainty if she'd go confront her uncle or not. He was another part of her past that she'd tried to overcome. He'd made her life hell after her father got locked up. He thought she should have kept her mouth shut, and he made his opinion known every chance he got.

With that in mind, I looked into her uncle, trying to learn all I could about him. Raymond Coleman, only brother to

Ron Coleman. Sixty-two, which made him the eldest brother. He'd lived in the house in North Riverdale for the last fourteen years, ever since Ron Coleman had been arrested.

I dug into social media, finding a Facebook profile with a picture of Raymond with his wife. His very *young* wife. Seems desire for youthful women ran in the family. Disgust settled over me as I scrolled through the photos of good ol' Ray and his wife. He wore the look of a man who liked control. Hard face, narrowed eyes. His wife had the look of an abused woman in almost every image and my hatred for Brie's family intensified.

I scrubbed my hands over my face. I'd been researching for over two hours, and I was starting to feel like a caged animal in this tiny room. I stood to glance out the window. Brie still hadn't returned.

Where the hell is she?

I should have followed her, but I hadn't trusted myself to keep my distance. I heaved a sigh and walked to the bathroom. Maybe a shower would wash away the tension.

As I stood under the spray, I let the heat seep into my muscles. My thoughts shifted from the information I'd poured over to Brie. I still couldn't believe she'd loved me and hadn't said a word. So much shit could've been avoided. The voice in my head scolded me for placing blame squarely on her shoulders. It wasn't entirely her fault. I hadn't told her how I'd felt either.

Once I was clean, I stepped out of the shower and wrapped a towel around my waist. The sound of a motorcycle caught my attention, and I strode to the window. The sight of Brie straddling the powerful machine had me hard in an instant. I allowed myself a moment to admire her on a purely physical level, and my desire ramped up.

Brie wasn't a woman I had to fantasize about because I'd

had her. Many times. I didn't have to conjure up pretend visions of what she would look like naked, writhing under me. I already knew.

I took my thick length in my hand and squeezed as I watched her walk from the bike to her room, hips swaying as she moved. An image of her bent over my bike, legs spread wide and pussy pink and dripping, surfaced. My hand tightened on my cock and I stroked, alternating between fast and slow pulls. I looked down, and instead of seeing reality, I saw my dick gliding in and out of Brie, her ass cheeks slapping against my pelvis as I thrust. Four strokes later, fireworks erupted, and my tingling arousal shot onto the towel that had fallen to the floor.

I braced my arm on the wall and leaned my head on it. I was spent. I had to be ten kinds of asshole to do what I just did. Anger at myself surfaced, and I pushed off the wall. I bent to retrieve the towel, and, on my way back to the bathroom to clean up, I heard my phone ring.

I snagged it off the bed and glanced at the screen. Adrenaline surged through me when Jackson's name displayed.

"Anything new?" I answered after the second ring.

"Hello to you too. And no, nothing much." Jackson's tone was stiff. "Have you talked to her yet?"

"No. I told you, I promised the BRB I'd give her a month and that's what I'm going to do." I blew out a frustrated breath. "Nothing new on Holcomb?"

"No priors. On the surface, he appears to be a model citizen."

My anger spiked at his words. "He's not a fucking *model citizen*! He kidnapped Brie and—"

"Goddammit, Griffin. Don't you think I know that?" Jackson's temper matched mine. "You know what I meant. He's got no record to speak of. But even more important than that, we haven't been able to find him. We've gone to his house, talked to his parents. They said he went to visit family in Texas and won't be back for a few weeks. We're keeping an eye on the house in case he returns early, but other than that, we wait. That's all we can do."

"Can't you have someone pick him up in Texas?"

"Based on what? Your illegal searches on the internet? Your identification? Do you really want him to walk on a technicality?"

"Fuck!"

"Listen, just keep doing what you're doing and as soon as you can, get her home. I still need a statement and for her to identify him. We'll get him, I promise."

"I'll get her there, and when I do, you better be prepared to do what needs done." After that parting shot, I hit the end button and stared at the screen, thinking about what to do next.

Nothing.

There was nothing to do but wait for the month I'd agreed to.

Twenty-fucking-three more days.

19

BRIE

"Thanks, Scott," I said as I walked through the gym door he held for me.

"No problem, Brie. See you tomorrow night."

Scott, the owner of the gym, had been letting me come in and workout after hours. He'd been working with me on my self-defense techniques. There had been a time when I'd taught self-defense classes, but my confidence had left me after being held captive, and Scott was helping me to build it back up.

I'd been in New York for a month, and every day got a little easier. Sure, I always felt like I was being watched, but I'd pushed past the terror that caused. I missed Indiana and the BRB and spent a lot of time reminding myself why I left. Despite honing my fighting skills and now being able to hold a conversation with someone, I knew I would never be the woman they wanted back. The woman Griffin thought he loved.

As I walked to Chaos, the sensation of being watched prickled along my spine. I picked up my pace as I reached a hand into the gym bag slung over my shoulder and palmed my gun. I didn't draw it out, but let it rest in my hand in an effort to bring me some measure of safety. It helped and I was able to make it the entire way to my bike without looking over my shoulder.

Before straddling Chaos, I stuck my pistol in the waistband of my jeans. I didn't want it to be too far out of reach while I drove. There were times, like this, when I wished I had the BRB as backup. But I forced myself to quickly move past those times because it'd been my choice to leave.

So far, my decision had worked out the way I'd hoped. I missed everyone like crazy, but it was easier for me to deal with my shit without them breathing down my neck. Without Griffin's declarations of love. Without the guilt.

I drove the short distance to the one-bedroom flat I'd rented two weeks ago. It was only a few blocks away, within walking distance, but I still didn't feel comfortable out alone at night. I parked Chaos in the parking garage across the street from my building. I scanned my surroundings and didn't notice anything that would cause my unease.

"You're imagining things." I wiped my sweaty palms down the length of my thighs.

I raced to the industrial apartment building, and when I crossed the threshold into the small space that was now my home, I slammed the door behind me and flipped the lock. The breath I'd been holding whooshed out of me at the sharp click of the deadbolt sliding into place.

I stared at the empty room, and sadness washed over me. I had no furniture, only an air mattress in the bedroom to sleep on. There were no pictures of friends or family, no knick-knacks, nothing to indicate that anyone lived here.

These were the times I missed the BRB most. With them, I'd never felt alone, even when I was the only one in the room. A shrink would have had a field day with my sparse existence. They would have likely pointed out that I was subconsciously not planning on staying. Putting down roots. And they'd have probably been right, but I refused to think about it right then.

I walked toward the shower and stripped as I went, leaving a trail of sweaty clothes on the floor. After the water reached the right temperature, I stepped in and let it cascade down my back. I was careful not to let it hit my stomach too much, the sting of a fresh tattoo still present. I looked down at the vivid reds and oranges of the phoenix that was emblazoned on my skin and remembered the vibration of the needle as it outlined the design.

It'd taken two sessions to complete, and during those endless hours, I'd made a vow to myself. I would treat the rest of my life like the phoenix I chose. Despite the hell I'd been through, I would overcome and never let anything stop me from rising from the ashes of my past.

Long after the water turned cold, I stepped from the shower and wrapped myself in a towel. I walked to the updated kitchen and grabbed a beer from the fridge and tossed the cap into the trash. I took a long drink and almost choked when there was a knock on my door.

I wasn't expecting anyone. Hell, there was no one to expect. Maybe it was Scott. Had I left something behind at the gym? I quickly dismissed that thought because Scott didn't know where I lived. Unease mixed in with confusion, and I chose to ignore whoever it was at the door.

The knocking persisted and grew in intensity. Whoever it was wasn't going away. I narrowed my eyes at the door, trying to mentally persuade the asshole to leave. When that didn't work, I marched to my bag and grabbed a white tank and shorts to throw on.

Halfway back to the door, I turned on a dime and returned to my bag. I grabbed my gun and shoved it in my waistband. *On second thought.* I retrieved the gun from my pants and clicked off the safety before returning it.

You're overreacting. It's probably just a pizza delivery at the wrong apartment... Or Steve coming to finish the—

Another knock interrupted my thoughts. I took several deep breaths before opening the door, a threat on the tip of my tongue.

All thought fled as I came face to face with an intense silvery gaze. I tried to slam the door closed, but a thick tattooed arm shot out, forcing the door back open. My throat constricted at the same time heat pooled between my thighs.

Damn him!

"Hello, Brie."

"Griffin," I murmured.

I stepped aside for him to enter. Really, there was no choice in the matter. I knew him well enough to know he wouldn't go away until he was damn good and ready. Might as well get it over with. The sooner I did, the sooner he would leave.

The already minuscule room shrank with the addition of his impressive frame. I watched as he turned in a circle to take everything in. Or rather, the lack of anything. My arms crossed over my chest and I absently tapped my foot on the concrete floor.

When he finally turned to face me again, his brow arched. "Problem?" His face was hard, unreadable. His posture mimicked mine, and I allowed myself a moment to study him before responding.

He really was a beautiful man. His eyes sparked with just a hint of anger, and his jaw was covered in stubble. He was wearing jeans that showed off his powerful thighs. The muscles in his arms bulged beneath his black T-shirt and cut.

"Brie."

My head snapped up at my name. *What the hell had he asked me?*

"Why are you here, Griffin?"

"Why are *you* here?" He returned.

Well, shit.

I should have known he'd turn the tables on me.

"Because… I… because…" I huffed out a breath and stomped past him, ignoring the zing of electricity that shot up my arm when I brushed against him.

"I'm not going anywhere, Brie."

I whirled on him.

"You have to." My teeth were clenched, and my chest was heaving.

"Why?" He was pushing me. Taunting me.

I had no answer to that. As angry as I was that he was here, a traitorous part of me was glad. And to be honest, I was surprised it had taken him this long.

My breathing shallowed as he took a few steps toward me. I backed up into the counter and put my hand up to stop his progress. Instead of halting, he reached out and grabbed my hand to pull me toward him. I collided with his chest, and his arms came around me.

I struggled against his hold. He let his hands drop to the counter, caging me in, and sighed. His eyes sought mine, and his stare held such heat that I had to avert my gaze to the floor.

"Look at me."

I shook my head and continued to stare at the floor.

"Brie." His tone held a hint of warning that made me shiver. "Baby, please."

And just that quick, the anger was back. I ducked under his arm and dodged his attempt to stop me. Once I was a safe distance away, at least for my hormones, I turned and glared at him.

"Why are you here?"

"To take you home."

"I am home." The words sounded false, even to my ears.

He snorted as he once again took a look around.

"It's better than the motel you were staying at, I'll give you that."

My eyes widened, and my hands balled into fists at my side. All of a sudden a puzzle piece fell into place. I hadn't been crazy. I *was* being watched.

"You were following me."

"Fuck yes, I was!" His anger was quickly becoming a match for my own. *Good.*

He started pacing. The room was so small he might as well have been turning in circles. I was getting dizzy just from following his movement.

"Stop!"

His body went rigid, and he slowly turned to face me.

"Let's just get this over with so you can leave."

"Is that what you want, Brie? For me to leave?" His nostrils flared, and his eyes narrowed.

"Yes… No," I sighed. "Shit, I don't know."

I walked to the counter and grabbed the beer I'd abandoned before I'd answered the door. I took a swig and grimaced when the warm brew entered my mouth. I tossed the almost full bottle into the sink, and against my better judgment, grabbed two more out of the fridge.

"Beer?" I held a longneck out to him, and when he ignored it, I set it on the counter. "Suit yourself."

I leaned against the island and watched the indecision cross his features. His forehead wrinkled, and his mouth opened and closed several times before he gave up and snatched up the discarded beer. He leaned next to me, so close our arms were touching.

"Why did you leave?"

"Does it matter?"

"It does to me. To the others." He turned and rested his forearm on the granite surface and rubbed slow circles on the back of my elbow. Goosebumps broke out over my flesh, betraying me.

"You said you loved me." There. I said it. I'd left because I was scared. Scared that I wasn't good enough or *whole* enough for him.

"I did say that." He leaned in until his cheek brushed mine. His breath tickled my ear and sent a jolt of pleasure straight to my core. "And I do." He nibbled on my neck, sending fire to every last nerve ending I had.

"You can't." I shivered from the sensations he was evoking. I was struggling to keep my mind on the fact that I wanted him to leave. My mind remembered, but my body forgot, and in that moment, my body was begging my common sense to go fuck itself.

"I can," he growled. In a lightning-quick move, he picked me up and set me on the cold granite. He spread my legs and stepped between them. The instant his erection brushed against my stomach, panic flooded my veins and I pushed against his chest.

He refused to budge but didn't push for more. His eyes searched mine, as if trying to determine if this was an act or if I was really scared.

"Are you afraid of me?" His eyes narrowed before he continued. "Or him?"

"Both," I whispered right before the dam broke.

20

GRIFFIN

*G*ut-wrenching sobs tore through Brie. It sounded like she was going to splinter into a million pieces, from the inside out. Everything in me screamed to tell her it would be okay. That I would fix it. But I couldn't fix what was wrong.

I could hold her, though.

"Let it out, baby."

I murmured this over and over while she was cocooned in my arms. My shirt was wet with her tears, but I didn't care. I had others. When her sobs slowed and became a wet hiccupping, I loosened my hold without letting go. I leaned back to look at her, and my heart cracked at the sight of her red-rimmed eyes, blotchy face and runny nose.

"Baby, maybe it's time to talk about it." Up until now I hadn't wanted to push, but it was clear that, while she had made progress, she hadn't really dealt with anything.

"I… I d-don't want… want to."

"I know you don't. But—" I slammed my mouth shut before I said too much. Pushed too hard.

"But what?" She swiped under her eyes and sniffled.

"But, have you really processed anything in the last month? Gotten over anything?"

She shrugged as she averted her gaze. Translation… no.

"Brie, it's just me. I know about your father. You trusted me with that. Why can't you trust me with this?"

"Because… because what my father did was tame compared to what *he* did." She spoke so softly I almost didn't hear her. I didn't say anything in hopes that she would let go of some details. She didn't disappoint.

"My father was bad. I mean, you know the shit he did to me. I thought I'd moved past all of that." She peered at me, and her blotchy cheeks flushed with remembrance of how I'd helped her.

I couldn't help the smirk that came over me, nor did I want to. I had helped her. But I'd taken as much as I'd given.

"Then I was taken."

She was looking at something beyond me, beyond the walls of her apartment. I tried to keep my body relaxed, but I'd seen what she looked like when we found her, and I couldn't help the fury that hit me like a freight train.

"I don't even remember how it happened. One minute, I was walking into the main house with Zach—"

"Ian." I snapped my mouth shut. This was her story to tell and who cared if she got a few details wrong? I sure as hell didn't.

"Right. Ian. Sorry."

"No, I'm sorry. You knew him as Zach, and it doesn't really matter anyway."

"Okay, so, the next thing I remember is waking up in that cave. I felt foggy, like I'd been drugged or something. Turns out, I had been."

She was silent for a few minutes, her face a controlled mask. If I didn't know any better, I'd think we were talking about what we had for dinner the night before. My blood boiled at the thought of her being drugged, incoherent, unable to protect herself. I stepped away because I didn't want the violence threatening to escape to scare her. Touch her.

"It was dark, cold, and lonely. God, it was lonely." She hopped off the counter and walked to the sink, giving me her back. "For a while, I thought you guys would show up. Rescue me. But you didn't." She whirled, giving me the first hint of emotion since she started. White-hot rage. "Where the fuck were you?" She yelled so loud I worried her neighbors would call the cops.

"Jesus, we looked. I never quit searching for you!" My temper spiked as feelings of inadequacy took hold.

"Not hard enough," she mumbled. She couldn't have hurt me more if she'd cut out my heart and tossed it in a woodchipper.

"Is that what you really think? That we gave up on you? That we just sat back and did nothing?"

When she didn't respond, I grabbed her by the arm and spun her to face me. Her eyes widened, and I knew I should back off, but reason was gone. Fury controlled my actions.

"Answer me." I shook her. Hard.

"Griffin, you're hurting me." Her eyes were huge and focused on my squeezing fingers.

"Fuck!" I pulled my hand back, as if I'd been burned, and walked away. I took several deep breaths before I could face her again.

"You wanted to know what happened, damn you! I can't control how I felt while it was happening. You asked for information. Well, asshole, you're gonna get every ugly fucking detail!"

As pissed off as I was, I took her yelling as a good sign. She was no longer shrinking from me, despite the fear she'd displayed a few moments earlier. She was angry and angry was good. Fuck, angry was great.

"You're right. Go on."

Before she did, she reached into the cabinet above the sink and pulled out a bottle of Jack Daniels. I should have known she'd have a stash. She opened it and took a healthy swallow before holding the bottle out to me. I shook my head, but she kept her arm extended, as if knowing I'd need the fortification to get through the rest of her story. I grabbed the bottle and tipped it back, letting the liquid slide down my throat and enjoying the burn. I handed it back to her, and she took another swig before she continued.

"I tried to fight. Escape. I mean, he wasn't a big man, and I just knew I could take him. I couldn't, though." She shook her head. "He was stronger than he looked. Or crazier, at least. I couldn't match his level of crazy, and eventually, I quit trying."

She paused to take two more swallows. My fists were clenched at my sides. I wanted another drink, but I was afraid the bottle would shatter if I held it. I fought an internal battle between going to her and maintaining my distance.

"Any time I tried to go against him, I was punished. Tortured." Her eyes glazed over and the mask was back in place.

"Fuck this." I gave up the fight and strode toward her.

She didn't resist when I framed her face with my hands, but she did flinch when I bent down and kissed her forehead. I let my lips linger a second longer than necessary, and when I pulled back, her irises reminded me of an erupting volcano. Despite knowing what would make her forget, I chose to do what would make her *want*. A kiss on her forehead was the quickest way to her heart, and I wanted that part of her more than her memories.

"Griffin, please." Her tone was breathless but guarded.

"Please, what?" My hands still caressed her face, the contact as necessary as breathing.

"Make me forget." Her pupils dilated, hinting at the lust that brewed just under the surface.

I wanted to do exactly that, but something held me back. Maybe it was the way she'd cowered from me just moments ago. Maybe it was the hesitation that was in her voice. Whatever it was, it screamed at me to take it slow and pay attention to every reaction she gave.

"Are you sure?" I needed her to know that I would always respect her boundaries, no matter how much my cock protested.

She nodded but averted her gaze. I gripped her chin and returned her stare to mine.

"Brie. I need to hear the words."

Please be sure.

"I'm sure," she whispered before running her tongue over her bottom lip.

My mouth crashed down on hers as my hands fisted in her hair, holding her close. She slanted her mouth, and her lips parted, granting my tongue access. I swallowed her moans and they lit my dick on fire.

Her hands shook as she tentatively ran them up my torso. I broke the kiss and trailed my lips over her chin and down to her neck. I released my grip on her hair and lowered my hands to her waist. She tried to push them away, but I wouldn't allow it. There was no one but her and me in the room, and I wasn't about to let her grant someone entry. Even if it was only in her head.

My fingers itched to touch bare skin. I slid her shirt up and halted when my large hands spanned her abdomen.

"What the—?" I reared back at the same time I tugged her shirt up to reveal the raised skin.

An amazing display of color covered her stomach. A

tattoo of a phoenix dipped below the waistband of her shorts, and its wings spanned the entirety of her rib cage. The head of the elegant bird was nestled between her breasts. I could no longer make out where the old scars were. It was beautiful. And so fucking sexy.

"I know it's big, but I—"

"It's fucking perfect." I interrupted her because whatever she had been about to say would've been nonsense.

I needed to see all of it, without her clothes messing up the view. I gripped the neck of her shirt and tore it from her body. Her eyes widened at the sound of ripping fabric. I pushed the ruined material off her shoulders and down her arms, letting it fall to the floor.

She tried to cross her arms over her chest, but I stopped her. Creases formed across her forehead, giving away her uncertainty.

"All you have to do is tell me to stop." I prayed she wouldn't, but if she did, I would stop. I'd have a severe case of blue balls and be in need of an ice bath, but I'd stop.

When she didn't ask the impossible of me, I let my gaze fall to the ink. I didn't rush my inspection of every line, every detail. After I'd committed every exquisite inch to memory, my eyes traveled to her pebbled nipples. They were begging to be touched, sucked.

My fingers found their way to her tits and lightly traced a path around her areolas. I tempted and teased, never quite reaching the spot her body was pleading with me to touch. Brie whimpered, begging as much as her body did, but I was enjoying it too much to rush.

Brie tentatively reached out and rubbed my cock through my jeans. The friction was a mixture of pleasure and pain. I paused my assault on her breasts to unbutton my jeans and tug down the zipper, giving her easier access. Her gaze snapped to my crotch, and her breath hitched. She slowly eased her hands into the waistband of my pants and boxer briefs. She hesitated for a second before she pushed both articles of clothing down my thighs until they pooled around my ankles.

I wasted no time shedding the rest of my clothes and kicking off my boots and socks. I stood before her, naked and throbbing. Brie's gaze roamed my body, and I felt like I was being lit on fire. Flames engulfed me when she dropped to her knees, and her tongue touched my tip. My cock jerked, craving more. She glanced up at me, and I took her chin in my hand.

"You don't have to do this."

Please, do this.

"I want to." Her gaze never wavered from mine. Her tongue wetted her lips before she continued. "He, uh… this is okay. I'm good."

That was all I needed to hear to forget my vow to take this slow. My hand fisted in her hair and maneuvered her mouth until it was perfectly lined up to take my cock. She parted her lips, and I tilted my hips forward, seeking contact. Her mouth wrapped around my sensitive head, and she sucked me deep.

My grip on her hair was forgotten, and my head fell back. Brie hummed as she milked me, and I felt every vibration as if it were its own separate touch. Her arms fell from my quaking thighs, and her hand cupped my balls. I was close to coming down her throat, but that's not how I wanted this to end.

"Brie." Her name came out on a growl.

"Mmm?"

Needing to come in her pussy, I pulled her to stand in front of me, her mouth releasing me with a wet pop. She had a sexy-as-fuck grin on her face. She was taunting me, tempting me, *torturing* me.

"Shorts. Off. Now." I pointed to the scrap of fabric that hid what I craved.

She obliged, but her movements were tentative. I studied her, searching for the panic. It wasn't there, thank God, but I wasn't sure how long that would last.

I lifted her up with one arm, and her legs wrapped around my hips. My boner was trapped between our bodies, and when her wet core rubbed against it, I almost lost it. Almost. My free hand twisted in her hair and tilted her head back, exposing her slender neck. As I carried her to the counter, I licked a path from the point below her ear to her collarbone.

Brie hissed when I laid her out on the cold granite.

"Sorry, baby. You'll warm up fast. I promise."

I spread her legs wide to accommodate my frame. I kept my eyes on hers, watching for her reaction, good or bad. When her pupils dilated, I trailed my finger through her slit. She was dripping for me. My thumb sought out her clit and rubbed circles around the bundle of nerves. Her hips bucked, and her head thrashed from side to side.

"You like that?"

She nodded frantically.

"Tell me."

"Ye... yes."

I speared her with a finger as I bent down and sucked her clit into my mouth. I added a second digit and finger fucked her while I continued to tease her sweet spot. Her knees drew tight to my ears, and I knew she was close. Too close. I abruptly stopped, and as I stood, I sucked my fingers clean, making sure she saw.

I took myself in my hand and let my tip skim her entrance. Panic surged through her, and she shot up off the counter so fast she would have fallen had I not been in front of her.

"I c-can't."

My cock protested the interruption, and I forced myself to take several deep breaths. My blood boiled at what she had inadvertently revealed.

"Did he…?" I couldn't finish the question. What was the point? I already had the answer.

She averted her gaze and nodded.

I saw red. I wanted to rage, punch something, kill him. But I did none of that.

"Brie, I'm so damn sorry."

"Can we, um…"

"What, baby? What do you want? I'll give you anything."

"I want to replace the nightmare."

"Okay." I wasn't exactly sure how to do that if her reaction to my dick barely touching her was any indication. "Tell me what to do."

After several false starts, she answered me with a suggestion I never saw coming.

"Can we, um, try a different position?"

My dick rejoiced, but my heart tripped. Was she suggesting a different position because she really wanted this, or was she just trying to force herself to do something she really didn't want to do?

"Is that what you really want?"

"Yes." Her hands flattened against my chest before she moved them up and onto my shoulders. "Please, Griffin. Give me something *good*."

I pulled her hands from my shoulders and laced my fingers with hers. My mouth fused with hers in a searing kiss. As our tongues danced, her body responded. I broke contact and lifted her off the counter.

"What are you doing?" she asked as I tugged her toward the bathroom.

"Trust me."

I shut the bathroom door behind us and moved to the shower. I adjusted the temperature of the water before picking Brie up and lifting her into the shower with me. I set her on her feet and kissed her again.

She kissed me back with more than just heat. My dick sprang to life, and I broke the kiss to spin her around.

"Put your hands on the wall."

She did as instructed, sticking her ass out for me. I grabbed the creamy globes and kneaded them as Brie glanced at me over her shoulder. None of her earlier panic was there.

I stepped forward at the same time I pulled her hips back and spread her ass cheeks. I let my thick shaft glide through her crack.

"Oh, God. Please," she begged.

"Please what?"

"Please fuck me."

I hesitated for a minute, giving her the chance to change her mind. She pushed her ass back even more, trying to take what I wasn't giving her.

"Hold on, baby."

I impaled her from behind. I didn't pull back immediately, letting her adjust. Her hips undulated, creating a dizzying friction, so I moved. Long, slow strokes morphed into frenzied thrusts.

"Harder, Griffin."

"Say it again." I slowed my pace, taunting her.

"Fuck me harder!"

"The other part. My name. Say my fucking name," I growled.

"Griffin. Fuck me harder, Griffin."

My hips flew. She reached behind her and dug her nails into my thigh, piercing the skin. Pain mixed with pleasure and I growled in her ear. "That's it, baby."

Her body shook and her pussy milked me. She screamed my name over and over as she came, and that's all it took. The tingling started in my spine and traveled to my balls. My release seemed endless as I filled her full of my cum.

My dick slid out of her as she crumbled. I wrapped her in my arms and lifted her out of the shower. I didn't bother with a towel as I carried her to the air mattress and laid her down. There was a soft blanket, so I pulled it over her body and went to grab a towel for myself.

"Where are you going?" her sleepy voice drawled.

"Just getting a towel."

"'Kay."

She was curled into a ball when I returned, sound asleep.

I spread out next to her and pulled her back into my body. As she slept, I went back over in my head the entire evening. The rage returned at the thought of what had been done to her. She mumbled in her sleep, and I forced myself to relax.

Tomorrow was soon enough for me to plan how I would avenge her.

21

BRIE

*S*unlight streamed through my bedroom window, and I flung an arm over my eyes to block it out. I really needed to get some curtains. *And furniture.* My body ached from spending my nights on an air mattress. I mentally ticked off the things I needed to purchase while I allowed myself to wake fully. As I cataloged the necessities for the living room, the smell of coffee hit my nose.

I bolted upright, wobbling a bit as I maneuvered over the deflating mattress. Once I gained my balance, I tiptoed to my bag to grab my gun. Whoever was in my apartment was about to get a nasty surprise, coffee or no coffee. I frantically dug for the pistol and when I came up empty, the events of last night slammed into me and knocked me on my ass.

What the fuck have I done?

Not what...who?

Resigned to the fact that I'd have to face him eventually, I stood to walk to the door. It was ajar, and before I crossed the threshold, I heard Griffin talking. I leaned forward hoping to catch some of the conversation.

"I'm gonna kill him... you didn't see the look on her

face… Jesus, I get it… I'll get her home… not yet… give me a few more days… later."

I forgot that I was trying to be quiet and stormed into the kitchen. The sight of Griffin standing there in nothing but his boxer briefs stopped me in my tracks. I took a moment to appreciate his sculpted ass as he was pouring a cup of coffee.

"Morning." He turned and thrust the steaming mug toward me. I ignored it. His brow arched as he looked me up and down. "You're, uh, gonna have to put some clothes on before you chew me out if you want me to hear a word you say."

I glanced down at myself, taking in my nakedness. My arms crossed over my breasts, but I remained frozen in place.

"Suit yourself. I like this view better anyway." He flashed a smile and tried again to hand me the mug.

That was all it took for me to snap out of it. I grabbed it from his hand and pivoted before going back to my room and slamming the door. Hard. The scorching liquid burned my throat as I took a drink and leaned back. How could I have let this happen? And who the hell had he been talking to? *Probably Micah.* That was the only thing that made sense.

I set the mug down on the floor while I threw on shorts and a T-shirt. I busied myself with nothing for several minutes, trying to regain some of the control I'd lost the moment I'd opened the door to see him on the other side. Before returning to face him, I detoured to the bathroom to give myself a little extra time. He wasn't going to make this easy, and I knew I would have to be firm.

I absolutely was not going anywhere with him.

Once I felt slightly more confident in my ability to stick to my plan, I went back out to the kitchen. Griffin was balancing a plate in one hand and shoveling eggs into his mouth with the other. Thank God he'd put on some jeans.

His chest remained bare, but at least his dick was better covered. Less temptation.

"Want some?" He spoke around a mouthful of food.

I wanted to tell him no, that he needed to leave, but my stomach growled, giving away the fact that I was starving. He must have heard the noise because he turned to grab a plate and scoop some eggs onto it. I hesitated before taking the plate he held out for me. The fork came next, and I snatched it from him.

We ate in silence. When he was done, he dropped his dishes in the sink and then just stood there and stared at me while I finished. I rushed through the last few bites, and after depositing my dishes with his, I turned on the water and waited for it to warm up. Might as well wash them.

"Brie?"

I jumped at the sound of my name. Griffin's hands settled on my shoulders, and tension twisted my muscles, causing me to stiffen.

He reached around me to shut off the faucet and then rested his palms on the counter, boxing me in. His breath coasted over my neck before he tugged the flimsy shirt off my shoulder and nipped my collarbone. I let my head fall to the side giving him better access.

While he nibbled and licked, he stepped closer and his erection pressed into my back. His hand caressed my stomach before sliding down the front of my shorts. He dipped a finger in my honey while his thumb teased my clit.

"Fucking drenched." The grit in his voice ramped up my need. "Come for me, baby." His free hand tweaked my nipple and then massaged away the sting.

"Griffin." My head dropped back with a breathy moan.

He leaned in and whispered in my ear. "Wanna fly?"

Incapable of speech, I nodded. The finger on my clit alternated between fast strokes and slow circles while the hand on my breast slid to my neck. Whimpers escaped me as he applied pressure. Every nerve ending buzzed and spots danced in my vision.

I rocked into his hand, and he slid two fingers into my dripping pussy. The sensation of being full, coupled with the squeezing at my throat, was sweet torture. My muscles sucked his fingers deeper, and I flew.

I was vaguely aware of Griffin's hand loosening its grip and him coaxing me to ride it out. After the convulsions of pleasure eased, I fell limp in his arms. He held me up until the shaking stopped and I was able to stand on my own. I turned to face him and extended my hands to the button of his jeans.

"This was just for you." His hands covered mine and brought them to his lips.

"But—"

"No buts." His eyes bore into mine. "We should probably talk."

"Asshole." I yanked my hands free and shoved past him to pace the room. "What was that? Soften me up with an orgasm before demanding I return home with you?"

"Is that really what you think?" He raised his voice and threaded his fingers through his hair in frustration.

A part of me knew I was being unfair to him. He'd never been that underhanded and I really didn't think that's what he'd done. But damn, I was angry. And hurt.

"That's not an answer." Judging by the look on his face, I was pushing it. Pushing him.

"Jesus. I love you! Isn't that reason enough?"

"You can't love me!" I screamed at him. "I'm not worth it."

He was in front of me in two long strides. He gripped my arms so hard I was afraid he would leave bruises.

"I'm a grown ass man, Brie. I love you. No matter how

hard you try to push me away, I will still love you." His breathing was heavy, but his face had softened.

In that moment, I realized something. I wasn't scared of him. I was terrified of what he was saying, but he'd proven one thing to me, time and time again.

He wasn't my father.

He wasn't Steve.

I believed him when he said he loved me. And the old me had loved him. But could this new version of me love him? There was only one way to find out.

Shock settled in his features as I leaned into him and pressed my cheek to his chest. His heartbeat quickened as I wrapped my arms around him. After a moment, he hugged me back, resting his chin on my head.

It was past time to jump in with both feet and at least pretend to be fearless, the way I used to be.

"Take me home, Griff."

22

GRIFFIN

We'd been traveling for two hours, and Brie has been stiff behind me the entire time. After a heated argument, Brie had agreed to let me drive Chaos while she straddled him behind me. I'd have to stop soon, otherwise she was going to be sore as hell by the time we got home. Maybe there'd be a place to eat where we could sit and talk. I'd have to keep an eye out.

When Brie had told me to take her home, I'd wasted no time. I was too afraid she would change her mind. It hadn't taken long to realize that all of our stuff wouldn't fit on Chaos, so we'd purchased a trailer to pull behind the bike. While I'd loaded everything up, Brie had called her landlord and somehow sweet-talked her way out of her lease. I'd have paid whatever the landlord wanted for her to break the contract but was glad it hadn't come to that.

I'd left the rental car on the street in front of the apartment after speaking to the rental place and had been assured that they would pick it up, for an additional fee of course. I wasn't sure that Brie wouldn't split if I left to return the vehicle, so after cursing out the guy on the phone, I'd recited my credit card number and paid the inflated three-hundred-dollar fee.

A sign boasting several restaurants appeared. One of them was a favorite of hers, so I nudged Brie with my elbow and pointed to it. She squeezed my side twice to tell me 'yes'. We'd developed this shorthand years ago.

After pulling off the highway, I drove toward Cracker Barrel and coasted into a parking space. Brie hopped off the bike to stretch her legs. I tugged my phone out of my pocket to check the time and noticed a few texts from Aiden.

The first two were updates on his case, but the last one had me narrowing my eyes.

"What's wrong?" Her question was hesitant, like she was waiting for something bad to happen.

"Nothing." I shoved my phone back in my pocket. "I'm starving. Let's go eat." I grabbed her hand to guide her to the door, but she planted her feet.

"Griff, this isn't going to work if you lie to me."

"Nothing's wrong, Brie." My eye twitched, and I prayed she'd missed it. That had always been how she could tell I wasn't being one hundred percent honest. I never outright lied, but sometimes I kept things to myself when maybe I shouldn't.

"You just lied again." She never did miss it. She crossed her arms over her chest, and my mouth watered. Her breasts were plump, and I would have run my tongue between her cleavage if we hadn't been standing in a damn parking lot. In broad daylight.

"Shit." I really didn't want to have this conversation now, but apparently it didn't matter what I wanted. "Aiden texted and asked me to let him know when we're getting close."

"Okay." She strung out the word like she didn't see what was wrong with that. Normally, nothing would have been. "So, what's the problem?"

"Jackson wants to be there when we get home."

"But I'm not—" I covered her mouth to silence her.

"I know you're not ready to talk to him, but, Brie, he *needs* your statement and identification of Steve." I took a deep breath before continuing because I knew she was going to freak out.

She didn't disappoint.

"How the fuck am I supposed to talk to Jackson when I can't even talk to you?" She was yelling and people were starting to stop and stare. I glared at all of them and silently thanked God when they moved on. "I can't do this. Take me back."

"No." I grabbed her hands and kissed her knuckles, one at a time. She relaxed bit by bit with each peck. "I'm not going to take you back. You're coming home. With me."

She huffed out a breath, ignoring my statement. "How have they not arrested him yet? I know you well enough to know that you sent that picture of me you found to Jackson. Wasn't that enough?"

"Yes, I did. And I managed to get a last name. But he skipped town." I held my finger over her lips to stop her interruption. "I know. It's fucking crap, but we'll get him. Together." Her expression was one of disbelief. "What? You thought I was just spewing shit back at your apartment? Baby, I meant what I said. I love you, and I'm in this with you. You don't have to do any of it alone."

"Yeah, okay." It wasn't exactly the declaration of love I wanted, but it was acceptance, and I could work with that.

"Can we go eat now? Please?"

Rather than answer, she started toward the door.

"You coming?" She glanced over her shoulder and caught me ogling her ass.

"Yep." I followed her but stayed a few steps behind. I loved the sway of her hips, and I wasn't going to pass up the chance to enjoy the show.

"Asshole." There was no heat in the insult, and she had a smirk on her face.

As much as I hated to admit it, she'd made progress this last month. It wasn't that I wanted her to remain stagnant and scared of life, but there was a part of me that was bitter that she'd had to leave to move forward. I'd never tell her that, though.

We had to wait twenty minutes for a table. Brie wandered through the little country store, never stopping long at any one item. Except for the candy. She wanted every piece of candy she saw, and I made a mental note to get some on our way out.

After we were seated, neither of us bothered with the menu. We always ordered the same thing, and today was no different. Brie played the peg game a few times and got pissed when I pulled it from her and beat her score.

Our food was delivered, and we ate for a few minutes before Brie broke the silence.

"Does everyone hate me?" She propped her elbow on the table and rested her chin in her palm.

"What?" My silverware clattered when it fell from my fingers. That was not a question I'd expected.

"I left." She shrugged and used her fork to push her food around on the plate. "We were a team. Now we're not."

"Your leaving doesn't mean the team isn't still there. And you will always be a part of that team." I picked up my spoon and pointed it at her. "You need to stop thinking like that. No one hates you."

"I just don't want anyone to be mad at me. I only left because I felt like I was suffocating."

I nodded at her to continue. I hoped if she kept talking she'd figure out how ridiculous some of her fears were.

"Everyone was trying so hard. Too hard. I didn't know what else to do. I couldn't be who everyone remembered. Hell, I still don't know if I can."

"And then I dropped a bomb on you."

"I'm still not sure I believe you'll stick around. Griff, there's a lot of shit you don't know. A lot that I'm not ready to talk about."

"You don't have to believe me. I have to prove it to you. And I will."

"I do know that you're not them. The men that made me this way. And you won't hurt me. Not on purpose, anyway. But I'm terrified that I'll hurt you."

"Did you mean it?" The question came out of left field, but it was the only one that I cared about the answer to and had been on my mind for over a month.

"Mean what?" She glanced down which told me she knew exactly what I was asking about. But I'd play if that's what she wanted.

"What you wrote? Did you mean it when you wrote that you loved me?"

She hesitated before looking back at me. Her eyes were bright with unshed tears, but she didn't let them fall.

"Yes."

"Do you still love me?"

"No... Yes... I don't know." She shook her head as if that would make the decision for her.

"I have an idea." I changed the subject so I wouldn't push her. I desperately wanted her to love me, but she had to come to that conclusion on her own. It would mean nothing if she didn't.

"Oh, God, what?"

"How about we drive a bit farther and then stop for the night? That'll give you a little more time to wrap your mind around going home."

"I thought Jackson was waiting."

"Fuck him. He can wait another day." The more I thought about it, the more I was warming up to the idea of one more night alone with her.

"Okay. Yeah, that sounds good."

I sent a quick text to let the others know the plan. Micah texted back right away, questioning my decision. A quick middle finger emoji later, and I pocketed my phone. He'd just have to trust me.

"Done. Now, let's finish so we can hit the road."

Brie relaxed after that, and we talked about other things while we ate. She asked about Micah's twins and everything else she had missed while Steve had her. There were times when she'd get a sad look on her face, but she was trying.

On the way out, I told her to grab whatever candy she wanted, and we ended up leaving with two bags of the shit. She always did have a sweet tooth. She may not realize it, but there were parts of the old Brie left.

We drove for another two hours before I had to stop. Her arms were loosely wrapped around my waist and her face was pressed into my back. Despite our jeans, the heat of her sex registered, and I struggled to focus. It was damn uncomfortable with a raging boner. I'd adjusted myself several times before I gave up, realizing the only thing that would help was her wet heat.

I pulled into a Hampton Inn and made quick work of getting a king suite with a jacuzzi. Might as well make the most of it. Not bothering to grab any of our stuff, I practically dragged Brie to the room, fuming when the key wouldn't work.

"Here. Let me try." She took the key out of my hand and unlocked the door on the first swipe.

I shoved the door open, pulled Brie over the threshold and slammed the door shut again.

"Griffin?" There was a question in her voice, but no hesitation.

"I need you. Now." I tore her clothes off, not bothering to be gentle. I spun her around to face the wall and held her wrists captive in one of mine above her head. I knew she wasn't comfortable facing me yet, and I needed this too bad to take it slow and help her through that.

I freed my dick before sliding a finger through her slit and stopping on her bundle of nerves. She was soaked and ready for me. I rubbed fast circles over her swollen nub, and my cocked jerked at the moans escaping her.

She glanced over her shoulder and purred, "Fuck me."

I didn't need to be told twice. I fisted myself and lined the tip up with her entrance, gliding it in her juices. Her moans grew louder until I couldn't stand it anymore.

I impaled her in one long, smooth stroke.

23

BRIE

Griffin absently trailed his fingertip up my torso before tracing circles around my nipples. My eyelids fluttered closed as I took in his touch.

"What's going through that head of yours?"

"Hmmm?" Electricity zinged through my system, making it hard to concentrate on anything.

He pulled his hand back, and my eyes snapped open. He chuckled at my reaction, obviously enjoying the effect he was having on me. He placed a kiss on my cheek before getting out of bed.

"Where are you going?" I scooted up the bed to lean against the headboard.

"To get our things from the bike."

I tracked his movement as he pulled on his jeans, sans boxers, and bent over to pick up his shirt. He shoved his arms through the sleeves and yanked it over his head. As he tugged the hem over his chest, then his abs, I silently bemoaned the fact that he'd covered up all that glorious flesh. He walked back to the bed and bent to kiss my forehead.

"I'll be right back."

"Don't forget the candy!" I called as the door closed behind him. His deep laugh filtered through the door and I smiled, glad that he'd heard me. It'd be a shame if he had to make two trips.

I climbed out of bed and went to the bathroom, grabbing my clothes along the way. I caught sight of my reflection in the mirror. *Holy shit!* My hair was mussed in that I've-just-been-fucked-five-ways-to-Sunday look. After I splashed water on my face, I finger-combed my locks. I slowly dressed and thought back over the last twenty-four hours.

When Griffin had shown up on my doorstep, I'd wanted nothing more than to push him away, make him leave. I'd been furious that he was there, but he'd worn me down. He always had been good at that. No matter what shit I flipped him, he never backed down. It could be incredibly annoying, but it was also kind of sweet.

Thoughts of all we'd been through brought back memories, some that I would cherish forever and others that were best forgotten. That first night together after we left the Quarterdeck: cherish. The numerous missions as Seals: best forgotten. Especially that last mission. We'd all been affected in different ways by it, but when all was said and done, the one person I'd wanted by my side had been Griffin. And he'd left. Like everyone else, he'd left.

I found myself getting angry, and by the time the key sounded in the lock, I was good and pissed.

"Got your candy." His words were punctuated by the door slamming shut.

I stomped out of the bathroom in time to see him tossing everything onto the bed. I stood there, hands on my hips, foot silently tapping on the carpet as I stared daggers at his back.

"What do you—" He turned to face me, different types of candy in each hand. "Did I miss something?"

"Why the hell did you leave?"

"I told you, I went to get our stuff." He said it almost like a question and looked at me like I'd lost my mind.

"Not now, asshole," I huffed as I walked toward him and grabbed the licorice out of his right hand. "Back then. After Kandahar?" I bit a piece of the red rope and chewed so hard my teeth ached.

"Oh." He broke eye contact and threaded his fingers through his hair. "I don't know." His eye twitched, giving away the lie.

"Don't you fucking dare lie to me." I was shouting now, but I didn't care. "I needed you."

"That's just it, Brie." His jaw clenched, and the contents of his left hand were thrown to the floor. "What about what I needed? Huh? Did you ever think about that?"

I opened my mouth to respond, with what I had no idea, but he put his hand up to stop me.

"No. It's my turn. You seem to hate talking anyway, unless it's to yell at me, so now you're going to shut up and listen. Do you think you can do that?"

My breath whooshed out of me, leaving me feeling deflated. Griffin had never yelled at me. I'd seen him pissed before, but it was always directed elsewhere. Before I could respond, one way or the other, he continued his rant.

"I've spent years, *years,* loving you. And for all I knew, it was completely one-sided. I've been there to help you through whatever it was you were dealing with, and I never complained. Not one fucking time. But after Kandahar, fuck, I couldn't do it. That was a clusterfuck of epic proportions, and I couldn't see past my own shit to help you." He was pacing, wearing tracks into the carpet as he spoke. "*I* fucking needed *you*, Brie."

"I didn't know." My tone matched his in both volume and intensity.

"Exactly. You didn't know. What's worse, you didn't even ask."

"That's not fair. You never said anything. How was I supposed to know?"

"Jesus, Brie. You're not this dumb. Do you think I fucked every girl I came across that had issues? That I helped everyone like I helped you?"

"Don't act like you were some kind of saint that never had other women. It's not like mine was the only bed you graced back then!"

"You're right. I fucked other women. But I never loved them. I tried, but you were it for me. God help me, you still are."

"You should have told me."

"When, Brie? Should I have said it that first night we were together? That would have gone over well. Or maybe I should have told you on one of our missions together. When we both could have been booted from the Navy. Oh wait," he snapped his fingers, "I've got it. I should have told you when you were banging every creep that showed any interest in you. Or even better, when you were fucking that douchebag, before you were kidnapped."

The crack of my palm connecting with his cheek reverberated throughout the room. His eyes widened as his hand flew to the mark I'd created.

"How dare you?" I said through clenched teeth. My shoulders were heaving as I tried to suck air into my lungs.

"Brie," he started, but I didn't let him finish. I stormed past him, grabbing the room key and the key for Chaos off the dresser.

"Where are you going?"

I ignored his question and walked out of the room, not once looking back. He talked about needing space, and he was going to get it. I worked to calm myself down enough to drive. When I reached Chaos, I unhooked the trailer and let it drop to the ground. I straddled my old friend and let the powerful vibrations center me.

I glanced toward the window of our room and saw Griffin standing there, hands against the glass. The light of the room illuminated him, and I could see the regret etched in his expression. I tore out of the parking lot, letting the wind whip away the hurt.

I drove around for hours, no destination in mind other than anywhere away from him. It was the middle of the night, and there was little to no traffic. Griffin's words played on a loop, and every once in a while, a tear would fall only to be quickly dried by the crisp night air. I hated him for it. Only...I didn't.

They say the truth hurts, and whoever the fuck they were, they're absolutely right. The truth had the power to knock a person down just when they thought they couldn't get any lower. And Griffin had only spoken the truth. My heart squeezed as an image of his face as he'd yelled at me filtered into my brain.

How could I have missed so much? Been so selfish? I'd been so afraid that what *I* had felt had been one-sided that I'd clearly missed what had been right in front of me. And what was worse than the truth? The realization that it didn't matter. It didn't change anything. I couldn't go back and fix my mistakes. I couldn't change what I went through and how it fucked me up.

I could only hope that, moving forward, I wouldn't repeat my mistakes. That I wouldn't push him further away than I already had. Is that what I wanted? To keep Griffin close?

Yes.

Was it purely selfish on my part?

Maybe.

Did I want it to be? Did I want to keep taking without giving anything in return?

Hell, no.

Without even realizing it, I'd driven back to the hotel. I pulled into the parking lot and sat there for a minute to gather my thoughts before going in to face him. Would he be angry with me? Worried? Would my outburst be the reason he walked away from me for good?

I took a deep breath and headed for the room.

There was only one way to find out, and I crossed my fingers as I unlocked the door, bracing myself for disappointment.

24

GRIFFIN

"She's been gone for four hours. What if she doesn't come back?"

Micah's sigh came through the phone, and it seeped into my bones. He was worried too. I knew I'd fucked up. I'd waited too long after Brie stormed out to place this call, afraid my latest fuck up would be the one that broke the tenuous trust everyone had in me.

"Did you call the police?"

"And say what?" I snorted. "'Hey officer, I fucked my woman against a wall then practically called her a slut and blamed her for her own kidnapping. She took off and hasn't come back.' I'm sure they'd be rushing to help. More likely, they'd find her and tell her to get as far away from me as she possibly can."

"You're being too hard on yourself, Griff. You're allowed to be angry with her. You're allowed to yell and argue. What she went through doesn't mean you aren't entitled to feel whatever it is you feel."

"Thank you, oh wise one." I was being a dick, but he let me. He knew my frustration wasn't aimed at him.

The key sounded in the door, and I spun around in time to see Brie stepping over the threshold, letting the door quietly click behind her. She started when she looked up and saw me standing there.

"She's back. Gotta go, man." I ended the call and tossed the phone on the bed. I stalked toward her, like a lion about to pounce, unsure of what I'd do when I reached her. "Don't ever do that again." As soon as the words were out, my mouth crashed down on hers.

Her arms came around me, and the kiss became more than just a kiss. Every thought, fear, emotion, poured into it until we were devouring each other. I didn't want to stop, but I pulled away to catch my breath, framing her face in my hands and touching her forehead with mine.

"I'm so damn sorry, baby."

"You have nothing to be sorry about." Her irises were flaming orbs of feeling, and she shook her head at my apology. "You were right. I was selfish."

"Right or wrong, I never should have brought up what happened. Not like I did anyway."

"Stop. Just stop." She broke contact and walked to the bed, plopping down on the soft white fluff of the covers. "Everyone has to stop tiptoeing around the issue. Me included. It hurts like hell to think about." She rubbed a fist over her heart. "But pretending it didn't happen doesn't make it any less real. And treating people as if I have the right to walk all over them because of what happened to me doesn't feel great either."

"We're a pair, aren't we?" I wrapped my arm around her shoulders as I sat down next to her.

"That's an understatement." She leaned into me, fitting perfectly into my side. "What now?"

"I don't know. Sex?" I was only half joking. Being this

close to her, no matter the circumstances, always had me painfully hard.

"Be serious." There was humor in her tone as she elbowed me in the ribs.

"I really don't know. I think we take it a day at a time. Fuck, an hour at a time if we have to. But," I tucked my chin and gripped hers, forcing her gaze to meet mine. "Whatever happens, we face it together."

"Together," she repeated.

"Brie, if there's one thing I figured out while I waited for you to come back, it was that we've wasted so much time being miserable because we thought we were alone."

"True." Her mouth opened wide with a yawn and her hand shot up to cover it.

"Come here." I scooted both of us further back on the bed so we could lay down. "Try to get some sleep. We've got a long day tomorrow."

"Not tired," she mumbled through another yawn. Stubborn women. "Griffin?"

"Yeah?"

"I'm sorry." Her arm went under my shirt and stretched across my stomach. She rolled toward me, pillowing her head on my shoulder.

"Shh, get some sleep."

"'Kay." And just like that, her body went lax and she was out.

∽

Fuck, that felt good. Silken heat wrapped around my cock, and I spiraled deeper into the sensation. When the vibration in my balls started, my eyes flew open and my head lifted from the pillow. I lifted the blanket to see Brie's head bobbing up and down as she sucked my dick. I thought I'd been having an epic wet dream, but reality was so much better.

Brie moaned and the vibrations continued. Watching as my length disappeared into her mouth was sexy as fuck. I couldn't take my eyes off the sight. I felt my tip hit the back of her throat, and when she swallowed, I came so hard my vision blurred. Once the pulsating eased, I reached down, grabbed under her arms and yanked her up to straddle me.

We'd fallen asleep fully clothed, but at some point, she'd stripped and somehow managed to get my pants off without waking me. Her pussy was hot against my shaft and it sprang to life again.

"Morning." She smiled a huge Cheshire Cat smile and darted her tongue out to lick my come off her lips.

"Morning, baby," I drawled. "Wanna ride?"

Her nostrils flared, and her eyes sparked as she vigorously nodded. She rose to her knees and took me in her hand, pumping my cock. I swiped a finger through her slit, letting her arousal coat it before trailing it to her clit. She threw her head back and slid down, taking me to the hilt. She braced herself against my chest, her arms stiff and her fingernails digging little half-moons into my pecs. Her eyes were closed, and her hips undulated.

"Look at me," I demanded. This was the first time we'd fucked face to face because she hadn't been able to before.

Her eyes snapped open, and the gold rings practically glowed. I increased the pressure on her clit, and she picked up her speed to match it. I gripped her hip to slow her down and was rewarded with a moan that came from deep within her.

"Griffin, please?" She was panting, chasing her orgasm.

"Please, what?"

"I need to come." She was pleading for it, and I found it impossible to deny her.

I pulled out of her and lifted her up until her pussy was above my face. I licked her folds, causing her body to tremble. I settled deeper into the mattress and gripped her hips to hold her still. I licked, sucked, and nipped. Each time I felt her getting close, I'd stop for a few seconds, drawing out the rapture.

I decided to end her torture and give her what she sought. I fucked her with my tongue, curling it inside of her. Then I finger fucked her while I drew her clit between my lips. She was so close. Her trembles became so intense, she was struggling to stay up over me. I inserted another finger, filling her up as much as I could, and she exploded with the added pressure. Her spasming walls sucked my fingers deeper as her back arched.

"Oh, God. Oh, fuck. Griffin." She rode out the waves of her orgasm before collapsing on top of me.

"Baby, we're not even close to done." I rolled her over so I was on top of her, and her eyes widened with panic and her body tensed. I sealed my lips to hers, giving her a taste of herself. I kept my eyes open so I could see her reaction. Her body relaxed slightly, and her eyes slid closed.

"Open your eyes," I commanded at the same time I glided into her wet heat, stopping when I was buried. They snapped open, but she looked away from me. "Brie, look at me."

She caught her lip between her teeth and slowly turned her gaze to collide with mine. I pulled out and thrust back in.

"It's just me."

I pulled out until only half of my head remained.

"I'm not him." I thrust in again, my balls slapping her ass. "Say it."

"You're not him." Her hips began to lift, and she matched me, thrust for thrust. "Griffin. Not him." Her words were breathy but determined.

"That's it. Come on, baby. Fuck me," I ground out through

gritted teeth. Her pussy gripped my cock, and I couldn't help but ram into her harder, faster. "Fuck, you feel good. I'm gonna come, baby. Come with me."

Her hands fisted the sheets, and she lifted her hips, positioning herself so I'd hit that sweet spot.

"Griffin...oh, God...I'm com—" My mouth caught her words, and my balls drew tight. As she milked my cock, I exploded.

"You're mine," I growled through my release. "All mine."

We collapsed in a heap, panting, sweaty. She pushed against my chest, and I rolled off of her. Our legs remained entwined and I wanted nothing more than to stay like that for the rest of the day, but reality called. Literally. My phone rang, and Brie grabbed it off the nightstand. Rather than hand it to me, she looked at the screen and answered the call.

"Hi, Micah," she answered. "Yeah, he's right here." She extended the phone to me.

"Put it on speaker, baby. I can't move." A blush crept up her neck as she did as I asked.

"I don't even want to know." There was laughter in his voice. Micah wasn't a stupid man. He knew exactly why I was tired. "Look, I hate to break up, well, whatever it is you were doing, but when are you coming home?"

"Be there this afternoon." I glanced at the clock to see if that was even possible and amended my statement. "Make that tonight." It was already ten-thirty. We had to check out by noon and had about five more hours to drive. Factor in bathroom breaks and food, it'd be seven or eight before we got there.

"Brie, you'll be with him?"

She nodded.

"He can't hear your head, baby," I whispered.

"Oh, um, yes. I'll be with him." She took a deep breath before continuing. "Is that okay?" I guess it didn't matter what I'd told her, she needed to hear for herself that she was still welcome. Still one of the team.

"What the hell kind of question is that? Of course, it's okay. You belong here. We miss you, kiddo." Micah's voice had gone thick, and he cleared his throat. "Besides, who's going to help me keep Griff's ass in line if you aren't here?"

Brie laughed at that, exactly like he'd intended her to. Micah wasn't one to tap into his emotions much, unless it was with Sadie, but everything that had happened with Brie? That shit had gotten to him.

"Jackson wants to talk to you. You okay with that, Brie?"

Her eyes snapped to mine. I mouthed the word 'together' as I grabbed her hand and squeezed.

"That's fine."

"Good. That's good. I'll hold off on calling him until you guys are here. Give you a chance to settle in a bit before bringing him out."

"Sounds good." She swallowed and I could see the indecision in her eyes. The fight or flight response was riding her hard, but she was a fighter. On the off chance I was wrong, she knew I'd just track her down again. I was banking on the fact that we'd reached some sort of understanding and it wouldn't come to that.

"Well, then, get your ass out of bed and hit the road."

"How'd you—?" she stammered.

"Brie, come on. It's me. Besides, I'd be doing the same damn thing if I were in Griff's shoes." With that, he ended the call.

Brie's mouth hung open and accusing eyes stared at me.

"What?"

"What have you told him?"

Shit.

"Uh, only what he needs to know."

"And what exactly has he needed to know?"

"That I love you?" It came out more as a question than a statement. "Let's grab a shower and get outta here." I rolled out of bed and strode toward the bathroom, giving her a view of my ass as I went.

"Griffin Strong, don't you dare walk away from me." She caught up to me and grabbed my arm, trying to spin me around. When I was facing her again, I cocked my head. "What does he know?"

I tugged her toward me, her breasts smashing into my chest.

"I love you." I swatted her ass and smirked when she let out a low moan at the sting. With that, I walked into the bathroom and stepped into the shower. "You gonna join me or what?" I called as steam began to fill the room.

The curtain was yanked to the side and she huffed as she stepped under the spray.

"Asshole."

25

BRIE

The strongest sense of déjà vu washed over me as we pulled onto BRB property. I took in the scenery much the way I had after I'd been held captive. *Captive.* I hated that word. It made me feel like a victim, and I was tired of being a victim.

The cabins looked the same, as did the landscape. I held on a little tighter as Griffin passed the main house and pointed the bike toward my cabin. I really wanted to be home, but there was something I needed to do first. I tapped Griffin on the shoulder, lightly so as not to startle him. He slowed Chaos and put his booted feet on the ground when we stopped.

"What's up? You okay?" He glanced over his shoulder at me.

"Can we go to the main house first? There's something I need to do."

"Whatever you want, baby."

He turned us around and parked in front of the main house. I climbed off the bike and stood there, staring at the structure that had once been my salvation. Griffin stepped up behind me, wrapping his arms around my waist.

"You don't have to do this." His breath skittered across my ear.

"Yes, I do." I turned in his arms and put my hands on his chest. "Together?"

"Together." His hands caught mine, and we stood there for a minute. He seemed to know that I needed a little extra push, so he spun me around and starting walking, tugging me along behind him.

When we reached the second step of the porch, the door swung open and Micah stepped out. The second he smiled at me, I flew into his arms and he spun me around.

"Welcome home, Brie." He set me down on my feet but didn't release me.

"You can let her go now, dickhead." Irritation laced Griffin's tone. I'd already caused enough problems between these two men, so I stepped out of Micah's hold.

"Is everyone else here? Aiden, Nell, Sadie?" There were a few things that I needed to say, and I preferred to say it only once.

"Sure are. Doc's here. So is his girlfriend, Emersyn. You remember her, right? She was the nurse who—" He stopped, slamming his mouth closed. His jaw hardened, and his eyes narrowed. I wasn't sure if his anger was at himself for bringing it up or at the memory. It didn't really matter which it was.

"I remember. She took care of me after... well, after." I looked back at Griffin, silently pleading with my eyes for him to be closer to me. He took the hint and came to stand next to me, his arm slung around my shoulders. I breathed a sigh of relief. "Can we go inside?"

Micah didn't answer, but he turned to go inside. Griffin and I followed, and he held my hand tightly in his. We headed toward the library, and when we entered, all chatter ceased. After a few silent, awkward minutes, Griffin spoke up.

"Stuff your eyes back in their sockets. It's just Brie."

It had the intended effect because the others all jumped up and came to me. One by one, the most important people in my life gave me hugs and welcomed me home. I didn't flinch or get scared. I hugged them back, fiercely. The last one in front of me was Sadie. She wrung her hands in front of her.

"I'm so damn sorry, Sadie. I had no idea." Tears welled in my eyes, and I swiped at the few that escaped down my cheeks.

Her face was a mirror of my own only she didn't wipe at the tears. She let them flow and flung herself at me.

"I'm the one who's sorry. He did what he did because of me. It's all my fault."

"No, it's not. I brought him to the house. It's my fault."

We blubbered back and forth until Micah and Griffin tugged us apart.

"It was neither one of your faults." Griffin pointed at each of us in turn. "Both of you, get that thought out of your head."

"He's right," Micah spoke up. "Ian was a fucking prick and he got what was coming to him." Micah turned to me. "Steve was a complete unknown variable that no one could have predicted. Those two *men*," he sneered the word, "are the only ones who have any claim on the blame."

I let the words settle in my mind. They were both right. What happened wasn't my fault, and it sure as hell wasn't Sadie's. It was theirs and theirs alone. I took a deep breath and faced the others.

"I need to tell you all a few things." I froze until Griffin's heat was at my back, silently supporting me. Encouraging me. "About me. About my past."

"You don't have to."

"Not necessary."

"You don't owe us anything."

Just the fact that they all really didn't expect me to tell them anything made me love them even more.

"I do. Maybe you don't need to hear it, but I need to tell it. I can't move on otherwise." That seemed to stop the protests. Each of them would walk through hell for me, and I hoped they felt the same way after I actually walked them through hell.

"Hold that thought." Griffin squeezed my shoulders before walking to the desk. "Micah, still got a stash in here?"

"Uh..." Micah hesitated as Sadie gave him an admonishing look.

"He thinks I don't know about it, but yes. Bottom left-hand drawer." She didn't look at Griffin as she spoke, but rather her eyes never left Micah. She wasn't really mad, but I remembered how she liked to give him a hard time.

Griffin pulled out the bottle of Fireball from the drawer and walked back to me with it.

"Here, take a swig." He uncapped the bottle and thrust it at me.

I did as instructed and then took another for good measure. I passed the bottle back to Griffin and he followed suit. We all took turns, and when the last person had chugged, I ended up with the bottle. I held on tight as I launched into my story.

"I, um, didn't have the best childhood. My father was abusive." Swig. "He always called me princess, and when I was young, it was fun. I was daddy's little princess. I mean, what girl doesn't want to feel like that? I always felt cherished, ya know? Like I was the most important thing in the world to him. But... but when I got older, it wasn't fun anymore. I was still his princess, but he was the king who ruled his kingdom with an iron fist."

Everyone had sat down by this point. Everyone except Griffin. He stood stiff at my side. He'd heard this story before, and he was as angry now as he had been that first time. I tipped the bottle up and downed another gulp. I passed the bottle to Griffin, and he passed it on after he took a sip.

"One night, when I was ten, I woke up to intense pain." I didn't need to go into details. The looks on their faces told me they knew what I meant. "It continued until I was seventeen."

"Where was your mother?" Nell interrupted.

"Don't know." I shrugged off the pain that question always caused. "She left when I was two. I don't blame her for leaving. My father was a monster. *Is* a monster. Anyway, that last night, he came into my room drunk. He'd never really been a drinker, so I'd been surprised." I lifted the hem of my shirt and showed them my tattoo. "I have scars. Lots of scars. You can't see them anymore, but I've got a bunch of cigarette burns." Several of them gasped. I glanced at Griffin, and his face was hard. Unreadable. "I thought that night would be like all the other times. Keep my mouth shut and pretend I was anywhere else but there. But I was wrong. He'd brought a friend with him, wanting to show off his *princess*." I sneered the last word before taking another drink of Fireball.

The liquid was seeping into my system, and I was grateful for it.

"Where's your father now?" Aiden seethed. Other than Griffin, he knew the most about me, but not this.

"He's in prison. I had him locked up, and he won't ever see the light of day again." I took great pleasure in that fact. "I went to see him in New York. Face my demons and all that." I waved my hand like I was talking about something mundane. "He was still as evil as ever. But ya know what? I've moved past that. He's not the demon that haunts me anymore." I took a deep breath. "Steve haunts me now."

"Baby, you don't have to tell us any more." Griffin was standing in front of me with his back to the others. His lips grazed my forehead before he wrapped me in a hug.

"Yes, I do. Please Griffin. Let me do this."

"Okay," he sighed. He stepped to my side but didn't touch me. He didn't know all of what happened, other than what little I'd already told him and what he gleaned from my reactions. I knew his anger was going to spike, and as much as I needed his touch, I gave him what he needed. The space to feel his fury without it touching me.

"The night of the barbecue, I was so excited for you guys to meet Zach." I stopped and glanced at Sadie. I hated that this part of the story would bring up painful memories, and I gave a curt nod to Micah when he stood and lifted her up to sit on his lap in the chair she was sitting in. "When we came into the house, I don't remember much, other than getting hit on the head. After that, lights out. I woke up in the cave where I was found."

I told them everything. Every ugly, horrid, embarrassing detail. With every word I spoke, it felt like I was living every day over again. By the time I was done, I was exhausted. Physically, mentally, emotionally. Griffin was pacing the room and the others' fury was like a living, breathing thing. Something I could reach out and touch.

"I'll kill him. And enjoy every second." Griffin's fist crashed through the wall, causing me to jump. "He has no idea what's fucking coming his way."

Blood dripped from his knuckles, onto the hardwood floor, and the sight did something to me. Took me to a place I never wanted to be again. The floor of that cave.

26

GRIFFIN

I saw red and it wasn't the blood dripping from my knuckles. My ears were ringing so loudly it took a minute for the others' words to register.

"Griffin, you either need to calm down or get the fuck out." That was Micah. I turned toward him, ready to smash his face in, and froze.

Aiden was on the floor, Brie's head cradled in his lap. She was limp and very pale.

"What the fuck happened?" I dropped to my knees next to her, pulling her from Aiden and onto my lap.

"She went down after you punched the wall." Aiden's voice was clipped, violent. I glared at him, unsure whether I was still mad at him or myself. "Get that look off your face. What did you want me to do? Leave her in a heap on the floor?"

"You both need to shut up." Doc stepped toward us, drilling us with an intense stare. "Let me check her over. Make sure she's okay." He checked her pulse. Lifted her lids and flashed a penlight to check her pupils. "She'll be fine.

Something triggered this, but I don't think it was medical." He pinned me with his gaze.

"You're sure?" When he nodded, I released a tense breath. So this had been my fault.

I stood with Brie in my arms and walked toward the door.

"Griffin?" Micah's voice stopped me, and I turned back to face him.

"Yeah, Mic?"

"Take her home in the Jeep. She needs to be in her own place." He pulled the keys out of his pocket and put them in the hand I had cradled under Brie's back. His hand went to my shoulder and squeezed. Hard. "And for God's sake, keep your fucking temper under control. Before I have to control it for you." With that, he turned his back on me and went to sit at his desk.

I said nothing. Just left, carrying the love of my life in my arms. The woman I'd scared so badly, she'd passed out. As I eased her into the back seat, I vowed to make it up to her. Again. I grabbed our things from the trailer behind Chaos and threw it all in the back, careful not to slam the back gate when I shut it.

When we got to her cabin, I lugged our belongings inside before carrying her in. I stood in her bedroom, in front of her bed, with her in my arms. When I bent to lay her down, I noticed the blood still dripping from my knuckles. *Shit.* I didn't want her to see that on her bed when she woke up, so I carried her back out to the couch and set her down so I could go clean my hands.

I flipped the light on in the bathroom and rummaged through her drawers until I found a bottle of hydrogen peroxide. I poured the antiseptic over the abrasions and watched as it bubbled the cuts clean. I repeated this several times before locating some gauze and tape to wrap my hands. Satisfied that there was no blood left for her to see, I returned to the living room. She was beginning to stir, so I knelt down next to the couch. I brushed strands of hair off her face and forced a smile when her gaze flicked to mine.

"What happened?" She tried to sit up as she spoke, but I gently guided her back down.

"You passed out." My tone was matter of fact. No hint of the turmoil in my gut leaked out.

"But, why?" She rubbed the wrinkles on her forehead, as if she'd be able to pull the answer out of her head. It must have worked because she stopped, and I saw the moment it hit her. "The blood. You were bleeding."

This time, I wasn't able to hold her down when she sat up. She swung her legs over the side of the couch and grabbed for my hands.

"You punched the wall. The blood started dripping, and all I saw was that cave. My blood dripping from my wrists." Her eyes got a faraway look in them, like she was back there again.

"Shhh, baby. You're safe. Look at me, Brie." When she did, her eyes focused until I was sure she was seeing me and only me. "I would never hurt you. I'm so sorry I scared you."

"I know that, Griff." Her hand flattened on my cheek and I leaned into it. "It wasn't you that scared me."

"Fuck, I want to kill that fucker for doing this to you." My anger was returning, so I forced myself to focus on her touch.

"Get in line." Malice dominated her tone.

"Baby, together. We can take him out together." I turned my head and kissed her palm. I trailed kisses over her wrist and up her arm. When I was met with T-shirt, I skipped her shoulder and nibbled her neck, over her jaw before finally capturing her lips.

She whimpered into my mouth, and I reveled in it. The

kiss wasn't our usual frantic dance. Rather, it was soft. Sweet. Full of promise.

Brie was the first to pull back.

"Let's go to bed." She stood and tugged me up off my knees and toward the bedroom.

I had a moment of panic about the blood, but she surprised me. When she saw it, she didn't say a word. She silently stripped everything off and threw it in the corner. I grabbed fresh sheets out of the linen closet in her hallway, and we made the bed together.

We each took our own clothes off and crawled under the covers, facing each other. Her hand gripped my cock and it sprang to life. I covered her fingers with mine.

"Can we… can I just hold you tonight?" I could've fucked her. Easily. All she had to do to turn me on was breathe, but tonight, I just needed her. In my arms.

Instead of responding, she rolled to her other side, scooting back until her ass molded perfectly to me. I threw my arm around her, flattening my palm against her stomach and curled around her.

"Love you, baby," I whispered when her breathing evened out.

∽

My body tingled with the sensation of being watched. I slowly peeled my eyes open and came face to face with beautiful fire-rimmed irises.

"Morning, beautiful."

"Morning." She was propped up on her elbow and smiling.

"How long have you been awake?" I tried to cover my yawn.

"Don't know. Twenty minutes, maybe."

"And you've just been staring at me the whole time?"

"Well, that and I texted Micah and told him to call Jackson. He should be here in about fifteen minutes."

"Jesus, woman. You couldn't have woken me up?" I threw the covers off of us, scooped her up, threw her over my shoulder and spanked her ass.

"Ouch," she complained. "That hurt."

"No, it didn't." I reached up to rub the spot I'd smacked. "You've robbed me of morning sex. And shower sex. You must be punished."

She was laughing as she struggled against the hold I had on her.

"Put me down."

"Gladly." I deposited her in the shower and turned the water on, thoroughly enjoying her squeals when the cold hit her skin.

"Fuck, that's cold." She wrapped her arms around herself and shivered. Her teeth started to chatter, and I felt an instant of remorse. Then she grabbed the showerhead and aimed it at my face.

I sputtered and all remorse fled. I growled as I stepped in behind her, yanking the showerhead out of her grasp.

"Baby, you're playing with fire."

"Promise?" She purred. Fucking minx.

"Later."

That seemed to satisfy her, and she started washing her hair. I did the same, and we took turns under the spray. Once done, we got out and finished dressing just in time to hear the knock at the door.

Brie tensed at the sound, and I dropped a kiss on her head before going to answer it. I threw it open to see Jackson and Micah standing on the porch.

"Come on in." I stepped back to allow them entry and

shut the door behind them. "Brie'll be out in a minute. She's just finishing getting ready. Can I get you anything?"

"I'm fine," Micah answered.

"Me too." Jackson looked around, taking in his surroundings.

"Hi, guys." Brie strolled into the room, acting a little too cheerful. "Why don't we go in the kitchen? Talk there?"

"Wherever you're most comfortable." Jackson was keeping his voice low and even.

We all sat down at the kitchen table, and Jackson pulled out a pad and pen, as well as a recorder. Brie's eyes zeroed in on them, and her cheerful demeanor crumbled. Now she looked like a deer in headlights. I squeezed her thigh under the table, letting her know I was there.

"So, uh, where do you want me to start?" Brie was fidgeting with her hands on the table and her voice was hushed.

"Can you tell me about your relationship with Ian McCord?" Jackson hit the record button.

"Who?" Brie's eyes narrowed in confusion, and then it was like a light bulb went off. "Oh, Zach. Right. Well, we dated for a little under a year. Nothing real serious I guess."

"Did you have any idea that he wasn't who he said he was?"

"Of course not." Brie's hands stilled on the table, and her eyes sparked. "Do you really think I would have continued to see him if I had?"

"Baby, no one thinks that. Jackson's just doing his job." I pinned Jackson with a glare. "Isn't that right?"

"That's right." Jackson's focus was solely on Brie. "Brie, I need you to remember that, although I'm your friend, I still have a job to do. I don't mean any disrespect by my questions." Jackson looked genuinely upset by the whole situation, and my respect for him rose a notch.

"Fine. What else do you want to know?" Brie was copping an attitude, but if that's what helped her through this, then I wasn't going to say a word about it.

Jackson slid a book across the table toward Brie, and as he did, his eyes cut to mine. I knew what was coming and I wanted to stop it. Protect her. But I couldn't.

"Brie, can you look through these photos and see if anyone stands out? See if you recognize Steve in any of them?" He opened the book as he spoke, and images of criminals jumped out at me. I immediately picked out Steve's photo and had to look away before the rage could take hold.

Brie tentatively reached out and pulled the photo lineup closer to her. I put my hand on her thigh under the table and squeezed. I couldn't make it better, but I could remind her that I was here. Brie stopped on several pictures and narrowed her eyes. She was tracing her finger along the page as she went, so when she would shake her head 'no', I had to force myself not to react. Not to praise her. At the ninth photo on the page, she pulled her hand back, as if she'd been burned. I felt her body start to shake under my hand.

"Th-that's him." Although she stuttered, she sounded confident. I knew she'd picked the right man, but if she wasn't sure, it wouldn't matter.

"Are you sure? That's the man that held you?"

Brie's head bobbed up and down in fast jerks.

"Good. That's good." Jackson pulled the book back to him and made a note on the page before returning his attention to Brie. "Are you okay to continue? I have a few more questions."

Brie visibly readied herself to keep going. She stiffened her spine and a mask of composure came over her face. "Yes. I'm fine."

"Okay. At any point during your relationship," Jackson hesitated on the last word, "did you meet Steve Holcomb?"

Brie was silent for a minute, lost in thought. Finally, she shook her head.

"So you have no idea how he and Ian may have known each other?" He didn't push Brie to answer out loud for the recorder. He simply wrote the answer down.

"No. None." She lifted her hands as she answered.

"Can you tell me about the time you spent with him?"

"Why don't you call it what it was, *Sheriff*? I didn't *spend time* with him. He fucking held me captive!"

"Right. Sorry." Jackson lowered his eyes to the table and took a deep breath before rephrasing his question. "Can you tell me about the time he held you captive?"

"It was hell. He drugged me. Said it was Etorphine, I think." Jackson scribbled that out on his pad. "Anyway, I tried to fight at first. I figured someone would find me, so I just had to hold out for a few hours. That turned into two hundred and twelve days." Her eyes glossed over as she remembered.

"The marks on the wall. That was...?" Jackson glanced from Brie to me.

"One mark for every day I was there. I only knew it was a new day when he would come *visit*." Her gaze hardened.

My hand tensed on her thigh, and I forced myself to relax. I looked at Micah, whose jaw was hard but his eyes held another emotion. Regret. I recognized it because I was feeling the same thing. We'd let her down. *I'd* let her down. And she had paid a high price.

"It wasn't your fault." Brie knew us well. She turned in her chair to face me and placed a hand on my arm and gave a reassuring squeeze before she turned to face Micah. "You either, Mic. I know you tried to find me."

Fuck, she was strong. Here she was recounting one of the most horrific things I'd ever heard, and she was comforting us. Fucking strong.

"Anyway, after a while, I gave up." She absently fingered the scars on her wrists. "It didn't take a genius to figure out that the more I fought, the worse it got."

Brie spent the next two hours recounting every detail about what Steve had done to her. By the time she was done, rage had settled in my gut like battery acid. What I hadn't known, I'd guessed, but my wildest dreams couldn't have prepared me for reality. Micah had long since abandoned his chair and was wearing a path in the hardwood, hands fisted at his sides, murder in his eyes.

"Is that enough? Can you arrest him now?" Tears had trailed down Brie's cheeks as she spoke, and she swiped them away now.

"Well," Jackson clicked off the recorder and shoved it in his jacket pocket as he stood. "That's the thing. We brought him in for questioning last night."

"And you're just telling us this now?" Micah whirled on Jackson, getting in his face.

"Now wait a damn minute," Jackson shot back. "I don't work for you. As the Sheriff, I was doing my job." Jackson sighed, and his tone calmed. "Yeah, as a friend, maybe I should have said something, but dammit, I don't want this investigation fucked up. If I had told you, I'd have been spending my day booking you assholes because you wouldn't have been able to stay away."

"Shit." Micah's anger deflated as he zeroed in on my expression. "Maybe you're right."

"Why are we still here?" I couldn't stand it anymore. How were we still talking about this and not acting? I was itching for violence, and my target was sitting in a jail cell with nowhere to hide from my wrath.

"He's being interrogated as we speak. Now that I have Brie's statement, I'm going to head in and confront him with it." Jackson turned to address Brie. "I know this is hard for you, and I'm sorry for that. If it helps, you gave me enough to bring him down."

"I want to be there." Brie's statement was met with incredulous stares from all three of us.

"Baby, you don't have to." I stepped in front of her and placed my hands on her shoulders. "Jackson's got this."

"I know he does. But," she chewed her lip as she struggled to come up with an explanation. "I need to do this. I can't explain it." She stepped around me and walked toward Jackson. "Please? I just... please?"

"If she goes, we all go." I needed to make my position on this clear.

"Fine," Jackson bit off. He pointed to both Micah and me. "But if either of you make trouble, so help me, I will throw your asses in a cell. Are we clear?"

"Crystal," Micah responded at the same time I muttered, "We'll see."

27

STEVE

"How many times do I have to tell you, I have no clue who Ian McCord or Brie Coleman are?"

I'd been sitting in this stupid interrogation room for hours. I glanced at the clock on the wall and was shocked to realize it had actually been sixteen hours. *Mama must be worried sick.*

I'd been on my way home from Texas when I'd been pulled over and cited for a broken taillight. The officer who'd written the ticket had then cuffed me, saying I was being detained for questioning in another unrelated incident.

At the time, I had no idea what he was talking about. After the questioning started, I knew exactly what they thought I did. Problem was, they had absolutely zero evidence. I'd kept an eye on Brie, and she'd given them nothing. She couldn't even talk. As long as I kept my story straight, I'd be home in time to watch Jeopardy with Mama.

"Care to explain why there's a photo of you leaving the area where Miss Coleman was being held?" The officer slid a grainy photo across the table and placed a finger on the man in the image. "That is you, correct?"

I pretended to inspect the photo carefully. Of course it was me. But I wasn't going to admit that. The photo wasn't clear enough to convince a jury, so why make it easier for them?

"Sorry, officer. I don't know who this man is, but it's not me." I locked eyes with the man sitting across from me and pasted a sad smile on my face. "I really do hope you can figure out who it is."

"Stop playing games." The officer's palms came crashing down on the table, rattling the glass of water I'd been given when I arrived. *Fools.* They weren't getting my fingerprints or DNA. No sir. "We know you were the one that held her in that shithole."

"Do you?" I challenged. "Why haven't you arrested me then?" A voice in my head told me to shut up, but I ignored it. I pushed to my feet and folded my hands in front of me. "Now, if you'll excuse me, I think I'll be going."

If it were possible, steam would have been billowing from the officer's ears. His face was red, and his jaw was hard. I smiled as I walked out of the room, gently pulling the door closed behind me.

I strolled down the hallway and whistled as I walked out of the building and down the steps. I felt confident that I wouldn't be back. As I said, they had nothing on me. Nothing concrete.

"Mr. Holcomb." I turned toward the sound of my name, and a fist slammed into my face. My head reared back, and my hands flew up to catch the flowing blood.

"Feel better?" A man dressed in a Sheriff's uniform asked the brute connected to the fist I'd just eaten.

"Much, thanks," the behemoth of a man responded. He shook his hand as if to rid himself of the contact he made with me.

"Good because that's the only shot you're getting. Do it

again and I'll cuff you. Understand?"

"Understood."

I stood there, staring at them in disbelief when I noticed two others standing behind them. I didn't recognize the man, but the woman? I could never forget that pretty face.

Well, shit.

"Steve Holcomb, you're under arrest for kidnapping, sexual assault, aggravated assault, and attempted murder. You have the right to remain silent—"

"I'm the one who was just assaulted!" I yelled as my arms were yanked behind my back and handcuffed. "Why isn't he under arrest?"

"Anything you say can and will be held against you in a court of law." My question went unanswered as he continued with my Miranda rights. "You have the right to an attorney. If you cannot afford an attorney, one will be appointed for you."

"This is insane. I didn't do anything."

"Do you understand your rights as I've said them?" The sheriff pulled me back up the steps and into the station. The others followed behind us but stayed silent.

"I understand that you're making a huge mistake. Like I told the other officer, I don't know anything. I haven't done anything."

"Uh, sir, what happened?" The officer who'd questioned me earlier was there to escort me back to the interrogation room.

"He tripped down the stairs," the sheriff said with a straight face. "Tried to catch him, but I wasn't quick enough." He shrugged as he spoke.

"Ah, well." The officer turned to me with a smirk. "You really should be more careful."

"I want an attorney."

"Cheryl, call Mr. Holcomb's attorney." The Sheriff spoke

to the plump woman sitting behind the reception desk. He turned to me and said, "What's his name?"

"I don't… I, uh…" I sputtered. I didn't have a damn attorney.

"Call the public defender's office. Tell them Mr. Holcomb needs representation and have them send someone."

"Sure thing, Sheriff." She dialed the number and leaned her elbow on the desk as if she was bored.

"Take him into room two." The sheriff shoved me to his counterpart. "I'll be there in a minute."

I was unceremoniously led to a different interrogation room than I'd been in earlier. This one had that two-way glass wall that you see in police dramas, and the table was in the center of the room rather than against the wall, with four chairs around it instead of two.

"Sit down." The officer shoved me into the chair.

"These cuffs are a bit uncomfortable. Can they be removed?" I knew it likely wouldn't happen, but I had to try.

Rather than answer, he took his key and unlocked the cuffs, then attached them to the arms of the chair. Wasn't what I'd asked for, but at least I could get some blood flow back into my hands.

I was left in the room alone and had no idea how long I sat there before a chubby, bald man in a wrinkled suit ambled in.

"Mr. Holcomb. I'm Stan Finley, your attorney." He sat down next to me and placed his briefcase on the table in front of him. He shuffled through some papers and finally pulled out a legal pad and pen. Turning to me, he said, "I understand you're charged with quite a few felonies. Is there anything you want to tell me before the sheriff comes in to question you?"

"I'm innocent."

"Of course." He cleared his throat as he made some notes

on the yellow paper.

I sat there, trying to come up with anything they might have against me. They had Brie. She could certainly bury me, but hopefully the attorney knew what he was doing. Maybe he could spin it so the jury thought she was crazy. Unstable. Hell, after what I'd put her through, she probably was. I smiled at the thought. Other than her, nothing came to mind.

The door opened, and the sheriff, along with Brie and the two goons that had been with them earlier, entered. Brie froze just inside the doorway and her face paled. My dick hardened at her reaction to me.

"Baby, he can't hurt you here." The man that hit me leaned in and spoke in her ear. He thought he was being quiet, but sound carried in the sparse room.

My attorney finally looked up from whatever it was he'd been writing and bristled when his gaze landed on the three non-law enforcement individuals.

"What is the meaning of this, Sheriff? It's highly inappropriate for them to be here." He puffed up his already bloated body and tried to inject some authority into his voice.

"I don't mind," I said. Maybe I was crazy, but I would thoroughly enjoy their reactions to this interrogation. Brie's reactions to me denying anything and everything they threw at me would be worth the intrusion.

"See, Mr. Finley, your client doesn't mind. Let's get started, shall we?" The sheriff pulled out a chair and sat. Brie sat next to him, and the two goons stood in the corner. They leaned against the wall and crossed their arms over their chests. Their alpha male routine was pathetic.

The sheriff placed a tape recorder on the table and hit a button.

Brie's voice filled the room, and even as the sound further ignited my desire, I became painfully aware of one thing.

I was screwed.

28

BRIE

Two months had passed since I sat across the table from Steve Holcomb. After being so close to him, I'd come home and immediately taken a shower to scrub all the evil off of me. It hadn't mattered that he hadn't touched me. I'd still *felt* him. Griffin had to forcefully drag me out of the shower to get me to stop.

Steve was currently sitting in a cell in town awaiting his trial. Any time fear or panic hit, I reminded myself that he couldn't get to me. He was being held under lock and key. Besides, I had the BRB to back me up.

Griffin and I were taking things a day at a time, and I finally had to force him to go back to his own cabin. It's not that I didn't want to be with him, but I needed to figure out how to be on my own. He'd been pissed, but he'd calmed down after a few days. We didn't spend every night together, and I was happy with that. Not only did I need to figure out how to be on my own, we needed to figure out who we were together when it wasn't all about fucking.

"Brie," Nell's voice called from the door.

"In here." I finished drying the last dish and put it in the cupboard.

"Hey, you ready?" She breezed into the kitchen and flashed a cheeky grin. God, I'd missed my friends.

"Just about." I wiped my hands dry on the towel and grabbed my purse off the counter. "Okay, ready." We were almost to the Jeep before I asked, "Where's Sadie? Isn't she coming?"

"We're gonna pick her up on our way out. She had to finish feeding the babies."

"Ahh, motherhood." I chuckled. "When your tits become life-sustaining." I liked to give her a hard time, but in truth, I was jealous. I'd never thought about having kids before, but seeing her with the twins? Let's just say it makes a girl think. A lot. And then there was the way the men all turned into softies around them. Especially Griffin. So. Fucking. Hot.

"You okay?" Nell asked as she drove toward the main house.

"Great." I fanned my face at the image I'd conjured of Griffin's tattooed forearms cradling a baby. "Is it hot in here?"

"Only in your mind." Nell chuckled and cranked up the AC.

We had to wait a few minutes for Sadie, but once we were on the road, I let the images go and really settled in to enjoy the day. We were going shopping since I couldn't stand to look at any of my old clothes. I'd been making do with what I could borrow from the girls and whatever clothes of Griffin's I confiscated, but it was time to splurge.

"Are you looking for anything in particular?" Sadie asked from her place in the back seat.

"A little of everything, I guess. I do have something specific I want to look for though." I turned in my seat so I could see both of them.

"Oooh, do tell." Sadie's face grew excited. She'd really come out of her shell since that night Micah had found her. "I hope it's something sexy."

Nell burst out laughing, and I feigned insult. "Sorry to burst your bubble, honey, but Brie doesn't do the kind of sexy you're probably picturing."

She was right, to a point. I liked to look sexy, but my scars had always held me back from some of the skimpier things I would have liked. Not anymore, though. Before I could correct Nell, my phone beeped from my bag. I pulled it out and looked at the screen.

Griffin: Have fun today.

I smiled at the little smiley face emoji at the end and shot a quick text back.

Me: I will. You be careful.

He was going out with the others on a new case. It wasn't that this case was more dangerous than any other we took on, but I still worried.

Griffin: I'm always careful. Call me later?

Me: K.

Griffin: Love you XOXO

Me: xo

I dropped my phone back in my purse and sighed. I knew he was waiting for me to say those three little words back, but I couldn't. Not yet.

I shoved my wayward thoughts to the back of my mind and refocused on the day ahead.

"I take it that was Griff?" Nell glanced at me before returning her gaze to the road.

"Yeah." I left it at that. The fact that everyone knew we were a couple was still a little weird. I'd spent so much time thinking that a relationship with him was forbidden. Old habits and all that.

"Back to shopping." Sadie leaned as far forward as her seatbelt would allow. "What is it you want to look for?"

"Well, I think it's time for me to actually start living again." I'd made great progress, but I still didn't go out with them on the weekends and since Griffin rarely left my side, I felt bad for his lack of fun. Besides, we used to go every weekend and I missed it. "Maybe we could go to Dusty's next weekend?"

"Yes, girl." Nell held her hand up for a high-five. I laughed as I obliged.

"It's about time." Sadie pulled out her phone, and within minutes, she was showing me pictures of outfits she had in mind, most of which I rejected for being too conservative. "What about this one?" She turned the phone for me to see her fourth option.

I grabbed the phone and stared at the woman in the photo. She was wearing skin-tight jeans with perfectly placed rips on the thighs. The halter was made of barely-there leather triangles and when I swiped to the left, I saw the image of the tied back with a whole lot of skin showing. Her feet were encased in red spiked heels that I knew I would struggle to walk in but didn't care. A chunky red bracelet set off the entire ensemble. It was perfect.

"That's it," I exclaimed as I handed the phone back to her.

"Griffin's going to lose his mind when he sees you in this."

"Exactly."

By the time we were done shopping, I not only had a version of the outfit in the photo, I also had eight more bags full of clothes and lingerie. I'd let them talk me into quite a few less practical items, but it was worth it.

When we pulled into the driveway later that evening, I was exhausted. I went inside and texted Griffin, letting him know I was home. He'd responded that he'd be 'right over'.

As I was putting everything away, I heard his loud knock on the door just before he called out to me.

"In the bedroom," I yelled back. I shoved the bag with my *fuck me outfit,* as Nell had dubbed it, under the bed and whirled around when I felt his hand on my back.

"What's that?" He bent to reach under the bed, so I jumped on his back and tackled him to the floor.

"It's nothing." *Smooth, Brie. Real smooth.*

"Uh, okay." He flipped us over and straddled my hips. His lips brushed mine in a feather-light kiss. "Did you have fun today?"

"So much fun." My voice was breathless, as it often was any time he kissed me. My tongue darted out and licked the spot where his lips had just been.

"Fuck, baby. You're killing me." His hands trailed up my sides, under my shirt and settled on my breasts.

"Hold that thought." I pushed at his hands, and he groaned.

"You're no fun," he pouted as I struggled to sit up. Not an easy thing to do with him sitting on me.

"I know, but I have to ask you something."

He stood and stuck his hand out for me to grab. When I did, he yanked me up and I slammed into his chest, dumbstruck. He smelled so damn good. I inhaled everything that was *Griffin* into my lungs.

"Brie? You had a question?" There was amusement in his voice.

"Oh, right." I took a few steps back, hoping to minimize the distraction. "Do you ever wish we went out more? Like we used to?"

"What? Where's this coming from?" Concern etched into the lines of his forehead. "You know I'm happy with whatever we do."

"I know that. But, we used to go to Dusty's and spend time with everyone else. Now, we either hang out here or your place, and I just feel like… I don't know, I'm holding you back from really having fun."

"Baby, no." He was on me in a flash. Not in a sexual way, but in that way of his where he made me feel loved. Safe. He blew out a breath, and it tickled my scalp. "I mean, I'd love to go out with everyone, but only if you want to. I know you're still not a hundred percent, and that's okay."

"But, what if I want to go out?" I eased away from him to look up at his face.

"Is that what you want?"

"So bad," I said on an exhale. "I want to go out with our friends. The way we used to. I want to live a little. Let loose and forget everything else."

"Okay, baby."

"Good." I gave him the biggest grin I could manage. "We're all going to Dusty's next weekend."

He doubled over laughing. I pretended to pout, but that only increased the hilarity for him.

"You are incredible," he said when he finally got control of himself. "Only you could have me so fucking worried one minute and laughing uncontrollably the next."

"Thank you. I think." I went back to putting my purchases away, careful not to glance toward the bag under the bed. I was hoping he'd forgotten about it.

"So, what do you have in mind for tonight?" Griffin walked toward me as he spoke.

I was standing at my dresser when his arms came around me. His lips caressed my neck, and I tilted my head to grant him better access.

"I, uh…" What did I have in mind? I couldn't focus when he was doing those delicious things to my skin. "Nothing much."

"I can think of a few things to pass the time." He ground his erection into my ass as he continued. He pushed my shirt off my shoulder and nipped at my collarbone.

"Mmmm." I wasn't capable of speech at the moment.

"But," he said as he stepped away from me. "Dinner first." He swatted my ass before he walked out of the room.

"Asshole," I called after him and heard him chuckle in response.

29

GRIFFIN

"I can't wait for you to see what she bought."

Sadie's excitement was palpable. I laughed at the expression on her face, and not for the first time since arriving at the main house, I adjusted the bulge in my pants. She and Nell kept hinting at what Brie would be wearing, and I was quickly becoming uncomfortable.

"Give the man a break, sweetness." Micah wrapped his arms around Sadie and nipped at her ear.

"Fuck, man. Save that shit for the bedroom." Aiden threw a towel at them, but Micah caught it easily.

I'd missed this. Being with the team and having fun. It seemed that it had been one nightmare after another for so long, but things were slowly returning to normal.

"You're just jealous because you don't have pussy of your own tonight." I threw my head back and laughed when Aiden flipped me off.

"You guys are pigs. Griff, do you talk to Brie like that?" Nell was standing there with her hip cocked, an indignant expression on her face.

"No, he doesn't."

I whipped my head around at the sound of Brie's voice and swallowed my tongue. *Fuck me.* I'd always thought Brie was sexy, but in that outfit, she was a walking wet dream.

"Damn, girl. You clean up nice." Aiden punctuated his statement with a whistle. "Griff? Cat got your tongue?" He slapped me on the back, and I shoved him. Hard.

"Well?" Brie looked at me, and when I didn't say anything, her face fell. "I, um, I'll go change." She started to turn around and my feet suddenly became unglued from their spot on the floor.

I grabbed her arm and spun her around. The instant she was facing me, my lips crashed down on hers in a bruising kiss. She was hesitant at first, but I coaxed her lips apart with my tongue, and she gave as good as she got.

The catcalls and whistles from the others pulled me back to reality, and I forced myself to end the kiss. I walked a slow circle around her, taking in every sweet inch. She was in ripped jeans that hugged her curves and left nothing to the imagination. Her leather halter top ended just below her breasts and showcased her cleavage perfectly. It was held together by two ties: one at her neck and the other about midway across her back. Her heels and jewelry complimented the phoenix tattoo as if they were meant to be together.

"You guys go without us." I didn't bother looking at anyone else. I only had eyes for Brie and her fuckable body. "Let's go." I grabbed her hand and tugged her toward the door.

"Keep it in your pants." She dug her heels in and wouldn't budge. "We're going to the bar. You can fuck me later."

"Baby, count on it, but I'm more worried about the skulls I'll have to crack at the bar." I popped my knuckles as I spoke.

"Not a man in that place will be able to take their eyes off of you, and I don't share."

"Jesus, there will be no skull cracking." Micah could say what he wanted, but I remembered when he'd almost lost his shit when Sadie had dressed to kill and went to Dusty's. At the time, I thought it was hilarious. Now, I felt his pain.

"Let's go." Brie grabbed my hand and guided me outside. The rest of the team followed.

Brie and I rode together on Amina, and the rest were in the Jeep. We always took the Jeep when we went drinking. You never knew when we'd all have to pile in.

It was pure torture having Brie wrapped around me, holding on while I drove. Several times I had to stop myself from turning off some back road and fucking her senseless. The only thing that stopped me was knowing how much she wanted to go out tonight.

As I got off the bike, I shook my legs, hoping to gain some blood flow. At the moment, all the blood I had was in my dick.

"You're impossible." Brie shook her head at me, laughter dancing in her eyes.

"You try doing anything with a steel pipe between your legs," I complained.

"Later." There was promise in her tone, and it did nothing to ease the situation in my pants.

"Baby, you have no idea the fire you're playing with."

"Oh no?" She waggled her eyebrows.

"Not a fucking clue." I adjusted myself one last time. "Come on, minx. The others are waiting."

The first thing Brie did once inside was order shots of Jack Daniels for everyone. She downed hers quickly, and in the span of thirty minutes, she'd had four shots and was working on her fifth. I was only allowing myself two beers since I was driving, but I didn't dare slow her down. She was having too much fun.

I watched as she danced with the girls to song after song, swaying her hips with the rhythm of whatever was belting out of the jukebox. Several guys tried to make a pass at her, but she deflected every one of them.

It took all of my willpower not to step in, but as long as she wasn't panicking or giving off a scared vibe, I let her handle it. She needed to trust in her ability to stand up for herself and what better setting to let her do it in? I was here if she needed me, but so far, she hadn't.

After a few hours of watching her let loose, I went to the jukebox and selected a slow song. When the melody floated through the bar, I sidled up to her on the dance floor, enjoying the squeal that came out of her when I pulled her close. The way my body responded made me second guess my decision to be this close to her in public.

With her pressed against me, the scent of her shampoo filled my senses. I inhaled several times, and my cock strained against my zipper.

"Stop sniffing my hair." She giggled as her hands went into my back pockets and squeezed. She let her head rest on my chest. "It's creepy."

I took a step back and looked down into her eyes. "If it's so creepy, why are your eyes practically begging me to fuck you, right here, right now?"

"I'm... we're not..." she stuttered.

"Close your mouth, baby." I tugged her back to me and wrapped my arms around her, dipping my mouth to just below her ear. "You can open it later, and I'll fill it up. Just the way you like it."

"Promise?" The word came out on a whisper.

"Always." I smiled into her hair.

She settled back into me, and the rest of the dance was a

blur. The song was over too soon, and I reluctantly stepped away. As I was walking toward the bar, my phone vibrated in my pocket. When I glanced at the screen, my blood boiled.

Unknown: Are you enjoying your whore?

What the fuck? I scanned the crowd looking for anyone that posed a threat.

"What's up?" Micah shoved away from the bar when I got closer, concern etched into his features. I didn't bother to question how he knew something was wrong. One look at me and he'd known.

I flipped the phone around so he and Aiden could read the text.

"Jesus Christ." Aiden's tone was laced with venom. "Who the fuck would send this?"

"I don't know. Ian's in prison. Steve's locked up." I shot off a quick text to Jackson to make sure both were still where they were supposed to be. I didn't think it was likely, but I had to be sure.

"Shit, we can't catch a break." Micah was fuming.

"What's wrong?" Brie had somehow managed to sneak up behind me. I went back over what was said, hoping it was nothing to scare her.

"Nothing, baby."

"Griffin, no lies. I can tell something's wrong. Tell me."

I knew she wouldn't let it go so I showed her the message. Her face paled but only for a split second before it turned red.

"Who the fuck would do this?" She was mad. Good. Mad was good.

"No idea." A text from Jackson came through.

Jackson: Locked up tight.

I breathed a sigh of relief and relayed the message.

"Let's get another round. I refuse to let anything screw up my buzz." Brie ordered another round of shots and I ignored mine. Not only did I have to drive, but I now had to be alert to any threat.

"Griffin, please. Try to relax." Her words were slurred, and she swayed. I hated that I was possibly ruining this for her, so I forced myself to chill.

"Sorry, baby. I'm good." I pasted on the best smile I could muster and hoped she believed me. When she didn't push, I figured I'd convinced her.

I managed to keep the fury buried for another few hours. When last call came, I mentally congratulated myself on not only surviving her fuck-me-now outfit but also for not letting my rage get the best of me.

As we walked to the bike, Brie stumbled a few times in the gravel parking lot before I finally scooped her up and carried her the rest of the way. After depositing her on Amina, the vibration of my cell started again.

Unknown: Better get your slut home.

Again, I scanned our surroundings and came up empty. The only other cars in the lot were our Jeep, a car belonging to one of Jackson's deputies, the bartender's beat up Focus and Dusty's pickup truck. None of the owners posed a threat. Hell, I knew all of them personally. I'd spent many nights at this bar drinking with them, but that didn't stop the feeling in my gut that I was missing something.

"Take me home, Griffin." Brie leaned over the bike and purred, "I need you."

All thought was instantly transferred to her, my gut feeling forgotten.

It was another torturous drive with her thighs gripping

mine. She spent half the time with her hands under the front of my shirt, teasing my skin with her fingertips. The other half she was breathing suggestive comments in my ear. It was a miracle we didn't wreck.

I pulled Amina in her driveway and parked in the garage. I threw my leg over the bike, and Brie followed suit. She wasn't as clumsy as she'd been at the bar and managed to keep her balance.

"Griffin?" She reached behind her back and tugged on one of the strings holding her shirt up.

"Hmm?" I couldn't take my eyes off of her.

"Fuck me." Her tits bounced free as the strings came loose.

My cocked strained against my zipper, and I unbuttoned them to relieve some of the pressure. I toed my boots off, slid my jeans down my thighs and kicked my legs free. Brie licked her lips as she took in the bulge behind my boxer briefs, and she took a step toward me.

"Stop." Her eyes widened at the command. She thought she was running this show, but she was about to learn how wrong she was. "Take three steps back." That would put her right where I wanted her.

I tore my shirt over my head as I stalked toward her. When I was mere inches from her, I noticed the ring of gold blazing in her eyes, and her nostrils flared. Her breath was coming in quick pants, and her hands trembled.

I removed my boxers and then took my time stripping Brie's pants down her tan legs. She stood before me in only a black lace thong and spiked heels. My dick jerked at the sight, and I quickly took myself in hand and pumped a few times. Brie's eyes darted to my hand and followed my movements. A tingling sensation crept up my spine, and I had to stop before I came anywhere else but her pussy.

"Baby, keep looking at it like that, and you'll be on your knees."

"O-okay."

"Ah, but that's not where I want you." I loved the feel of her lips wrapped around my cock, but I had something else in mind.

"Wh-where do you want me?"

Rather than answer, I tilted my head, pretending to think about it. I wanted her any which way I could have her, but I wanted her begging for it.

"Griffin, pl—"

I silenced her with a kiss. I nibbled on her bottom lip, and her tongue teased mine. Her hands were threaded in my hair, and she was trying to pull me closer. Any closer and we'd become one. I used my body to ease her toward the bike until her ass bumped the seat. I tore my lips from hers and moaned.

"I've always wanted to take you bent over my bike." I trailed a finger between her tits, down her belly until I reached the top of her panties. I slid the fabric aside and dipped a finger into her pussy.

"Fucking soaked." Never breaking eye contact, I brought the wet digit to my mouth and licked it clean.

"Griffin, fuck me," she begged.

"Not yet, baby."

"Please."

"Turn around." She spun around. "Bend over." She knew exactly what I wanted. The sight of her bent over Amina, the scrap of thong disappearing between her cheeks would be burned into my brain for eternity. "Fucking. Beautiful."

She peeked at me over her shoulder, and I shook my head at her. She whipped her head back around and lowered it.

"Spread your legs so I can see that glistening pussy." When she did, I almost came on the spot. "Are you ready for me?" Brie nodded as I let my cock tease her ass. I wrapped an arm around her and teased her clit. "I can't hear you."

"I'm ready."

"Ready for what?" I needed more from her.

"You," she breathed.

"I'm right here." I bent over her, shoving my cock between her cheeks to tantalize her tight hole while my finger tortured her clit. "What do you want from me?" I trailed my tongue down her spine and she shivered.

"You. I need you. Fuck me, Griffin."

"Yes, ma'am." I slid my cock into the velvet heat of her pussy and hissed. "So fucking tight." I stood back up so I could watch my dick disappear into her in long, slow strokes.

"Faster." She arched her back, tantalizing me even more with her ass.

"Brace yourself, baby." I grabbed a handlebar with one hand and fisted the other in her hair as I pistoned in and out of her. Brie screamed out in pleasure.

Sweat trailed down my back, and my legs started to shake. I was so damn close, and I wanted her to explode with me.

"Touch yourself, baby," I growled. Her hand went to her clit and she rubbed furiously as I thrust as hard and as fast as I could. "That's it, baby. Take me so damn good." Within seconds, she tightened around my cock and my balls drew up tight. We both shouted out our release before collapsing onto the bike.

Our bodies were slick, and our chests heaved. Afraid I would crush her, I levered myself up and slid out of her. I helped her stand and turned her to face me.

"Always so good," I said before giving her a quick, smacking kiss.

"Mmm." Her body leaned toward me when I stepped

away. I lifted her into my arms and carried her inside to deposit her limp body on her bed.

"I love you, Brie." I crawled under the covers with her and held her tight.

"Mmm," was her only response.

30

BRIE

"Any leads?" I'd just finished my post-workout shower and stood behind Griffin wrapped in a towel.

He was staring intently at his laptop. He'd been spending every free minute he had trying to trace the texts he'd been receiving. They'd started the night at Dusty's and hadn't stopped.

Rather than answer, he grunted, something he tended to do when he was engrossed in work. I leaned over him to nibble on his ear and smooth my hands over his chest.

"Not now, baby." He lifted one of my hands to his lips and pressed a quick kiss on my palm. "Sorry. I wanna work on this as long as I can before the storm hits."

"Fair enough." I was pouting, but I wasn't really mad. Griffin was right. He needed to focus, and there *was* a big storm coming. At least according to the weatherman. Indiana weather was so unpredictable, and we were as likely to get six inches of snow as we were to get severe thunderstorms.

As I blow-dried my hair, I thought over the last few weeks. Griffin had slept at my cabin ever since the night at

Dusty's. It wasn't something we talked about, but he'd slowly been bringing his things and leaving them here. First it was a change of clothes, then his toothbrush. Now his things occupied an entire drawer in my dresser and half my closet.

I loved it.

Get real. You love more than his things in your house.

My reflection stared back at me with wide eyes. Was that true? Did I love more than his things? Did I love him?

Yes.

The answer came fast and hard. My fingers gripped the edge of the bathroom countertop and my knees threatened to buckle.

"Holy shit. I love him." The woman in the mirror said nothing in return. "You're no help," I muttered.

"Who are you talking to?" Griffin's voice came through the door and I almost jumped out of my skin.

"Nobody." The word was clipped. "I'll be out in a minute."

"Hurry it up. I gotta drain the pipes."

I rolled my eyes at the expression that I'd become so used to hearing. It was amazing the things you never knew about a person until you practically lived together. I made him wait a little longer than a minute because, quite frankly, it took that long for me to be able to face him after my earlier revelation.

"'Bout time." He scooted around me when I opened the door and didn't even bother to close it behind him.

I dressed for comfort, in jeans and a camo tank. I didn't bother with shoes, since we weren't going anywhere. As I was making the bed, something buzzed. I glanced toward my phone on the nightstand and realized I was getting a text.

Unknown: Are you bored with him yet?

I jumped back at the same time I threw the phone on the

bed as if it had burned my fingertips. The phone buzzed several more times, and I took a tentative step forward, craning my neck to see the screen. I wasn't close enough to read anything, so I took another step, then another. I leaned toward the center of the bed where the phone was, and when my fingers grazed the device, I pulled them back. After two false tries, I grabbed the phone and plopped down on the bed. It took another several seconds for me to get up the nerve to look at the screen, and when I did, I screamed.

> **Unknown: I love that outfit. Not as much as I love the little number you had on last night.**
>
> **Unknown: Don't be afraid. The phone won't bite.**
>
> **Unknown: Where was this fear last night? You let him choke you like a dirty little whore.**

"What the fuck?" Griffin came barreling into the bedroom, slamming the door into the wall. His gun was drawn, and he scanned all four corners. When his eyes finally landed on me, confusion seeped into his gaze. "What's wrong?"

When I didn't answer, he moved closer to me. "Baby, what is it?" When I still didn't answer, he yanked the phone from my grasp and hit the button to light up the screen. "Son of a bitch."

"Who… who is… how are… what…?" I didn't know which question to ask first.

"Yeah, get Micah and get up here." His words shook me from my trance. He was putting his cell in his back pocket, and his gun was holstered. "Come here, baby." He pulled me up from the bed and circled his arms around me. "We'll figure this out. I promise."

"Griff, he, uh, he said he liked my outfit. And he knew what we did last night. How? How could—" I slapped my hand over my mouth, the answer hitting me before the question was even asked. I shoved out of Griffin's arms and scrambled to my feet on the bed.

"What are you doing?"

"Think about it." I inspected the ceiling fan, the light bulbs, running my hands over every inch. "He *saw* us. The only way to do that is if there are cameras."

"Motherfucker." He was on the bed next to me in a flash.

After a thorough search of the fan, we came up empty.

"It's gotta be here somewhere," I grumbled. "This is your wheelhouse, Griff. Where would you hide a camera?" My eyes pleaded with him for an answer.

He jumped off the bed and turned in slow circles, taking in the walls, corners, everything. After the third circle, he walked to the vent and bent to peer at it. As he inspected it, Micah and Aiden came running through the door.

"You sick fuck." Griffin pulled what appeared to be a shiny black pill from the vent cover and held it between his fingers.

"What the hell?" Aiden stepped in close to get a good look.

"That's some high tech shit. No way this is all Steve." Micah's voice was hard but sure. "I'm calling Jackson." While he did that, Griffin walked over and showed me the tiny camera.

"When the hell could he have done this?" I assumed it was Steve that had placed the privacy stealing device, but it made no sense. "I suppose he could have gotten in here while he had me but—"

"I was here." Griffin cut me off. "He couldn't have gotten in here then."

"Oh." That was a little tidbit that he, and everyone else,

had forgotten to mention. "Well, then, when?" I squeezed my throbbing temples in an effort to ease the headache that was forming.

"Jackson's on his way. He confirmed that both Steve and Ian are still locked up and neither have had access to a phone or computer, so it can't be them sending the texts." Micah looked at the camera and cursed a blue streak. "Jackson is bringing a crime scene crew to sweep the rest of the house."

The thought that there were more hadn't even crossed my mind before that moment. Now that it had, I fought the urge to jump back in the shower and scrub away the violation.

The guys methodically went through the house in search of more cameras. I stood back and watched, caught between wanting to know what they found and a deep-seated need to remain ignorant. By the time Jackson and his men got there, four more cameras were sitting on my kitchen table, taunting me with what they had seen.

"Brie, is there anyone else you can think of that could be behind this?" Jackson's eyes bore into mine, searching for an answer I didn't have. He and his team had searched the entire house and found six more cameras. They'd been everywhere. There'd been at least one in every room, if not two in some.

"No. There's no one." My shoulders rose and fell as I heaved a sigh. This was nuts. I'd never felt unsafe in my own home until I'd been taken. And now that I finally had a life again, it was crumbling around me. Maybe I should leave. Go back to New York. At least no one else would get hurt because of me.

"You're not going anywhere. Do you hear me?"

I hadn't realized I'd spoken aloud until Griffin spun me around and his hand grasped my chin.

"I... I won't leave."

"Promise me, Brie. Promise me you won't leave again." His grip was unforgiving, and his jaw was set.

"I promise." Even if I wanted to leave this place, I could never leave him again. Crazy as it was, I loved him.

You really need to tell him how you feel.

Later.

No. Now.

"Griff, can we…" My eyes darted around the room to see if the others were paying attention. "Can we go outside for a minute?"

"We're gonna take off," Jackson spoke up from behind me. When I faced him, he showed me the weather alert on his phone. "Looks like the weatherman wasn't completely off the mark this time. We need to get back in case it gets bad in town."

"Thanks for coming out, man." Griffin released his hold on me and shook Jackson's hand. "Let us know if you figure anything out."

"Sure thing." When he reached the door, he glanced back over his shoulder. "We got all the cameras, so you can relax for now. Tomorrow will be soon enough to sort this all out. Stay safe." His hand rose in a wave and then he was gone.

After that, I hadn't been able to sit still.

"Baby, come here." Griffin sat on the couch staring at me with a worried expression.

After everyone was gone, we'd tried to watch a movie, but I'd only made it through the first fifteen minutes before I got up to do the dishes. Not that there were a ton of them. It had taken me all of five minutes. After that, I'd gone from room to room, cleaning anything and everything I could. Anything to keep my mind off that morning's discoveries.

"I'm just going to do a load of laundry real quick." As I carried the laundry basket toward the little stackable washer and dryer in the hall closet, a clap of thunder rattled the cabin. I dropped the basket and screamed.

"Baby, it's just a storm. You love storms." Griffin was next to me in a second. He wrapped his arms around me before placing a kiss to my temple.

"That was before—" The lights flickered but remained on.

"Come on, let's go finish that movie. Maybe we'll get lucky and the power will stay on. And hey," he waggled his eyebrows at me, "if it doesn't, I can think of a few ways to make use of the dark."

I huffed out a breath, stomped to the couch, and threw myself down. It was all very dramatic and very unlike me, but I didn't care.

Griffin shook his head and chuckled. "You're adorable." I rolled my eyes as he came and sat next to me. He grabbed the remote and hit play before leaning back and maneuvering me between his legs so my back was resting on his chest.

"See, isn't that better?" He covered us with a blanket and let his hands roam. After a few minutes, my body relaxed and we were both asleep.

31

GRIFFIN

I jackknifed into a sitting position, coming awake with a start. The space between my legs was empty. Brie was gone.

"Brie," I yelled as I shot off the couch and ran to her bedroom. The wind whipped against the cabin, and a flash of lightning lit up the room. Empty. Seconds later, thunder boomed, rattling the house.

"I'm right here." Brie's voice startled me, and I whipped around to face her.

"Where were you?" The question came out angry, and I took a deep breath to cool my blood. I wasn't mad. I'd been terrified when I awoke alone.

"I was looking for these." She held up a few candles and a matchbook. "I woke up having to pee, and the power was out." She set a candle on the nightstand and lit it, shaking the flame out and tossing the match into the glass. When she turned to go to the door, she collided with my chest and her eyes rose to mine. "You okay?"

"Yeah." I threaded my fingers through her hair and gave

her a long, lingering kiss. "I am now," I said when we broke apart and my forehead rested against hers.

"Okay." She drew out the word, almost like she didn't believe me. "Help me with these?" She handed over the candles before stepping around me and disappearing from the room.

"Yes, ma'am," I muttered to the empty room. I stood there a moment, trying to slow my rapid heartbeat, when the sound of glass breaking shattered my hard-won calm.

"Brie?"

"Griffin?" Her call echoed mine.

"What was that?" I asked her when I reached the kitchen.

"It sounded like a window breaking." She started to walk away, and I grabbed her arm.

"Let me go check it out."

She bristled but didn't argue.

I checked the windows, one room at a time, and I was beginning to think we'd both lost our minds. Then I saw it. The jagged edges of broken glass in the spare room window. Rain was soaking the floor, and when lightning flashed, I caught sight of something.

"What the?" I bent down to see a rock with a note duct-taped to it. I unfolded the piece of paper and my blood boiled.

I'm coming for her.

"Brie," I yelled as I stood up. Rain pelted my face through the broken glass, and the cold wind whipped against my body. I was about to yell her name again when something crashed into my skull.

"Brie." Her name fell from my lips as I went down, first to my knees and then flat on my stomach. I tried to hold on to consciousness, but I lost the fight as my world went dark.

∽

"Let me go, motherfucker!" Brie's voice muffled as if I was submerged in water.

Someone had put weights on my eyelids, and my head throbbed.

What the fuck?

It took every ounce of strength I had to open my eyes, and when I did, adrenaline surged through me, and I thrashed against the ropes at my wrists and ankles.

"Get your fucking hands off her." I continued to struggle against the binds, but it was useless.

Brie was being held down on the bed by two men, both of whom I recognized and both of whom I was completely shocked to see. Steve stood at the foot of the bed, and near her head was one of Jackson's deputies.

Shit. What was his name?

"Carter." His name finally clicked. "What the hell?"

"Well, well, well. Look who finally woke up." Steve's voice was low, menacing, crazy. "Not so big and bad now, are ya?" He finished clicking the handcuffs into place around her ankles.

Brie's eyes caught mine, and she kicked and bucked. The terror I saw there slayed me. I fought the ropes harder but still couldn't break free.

"Come on, Steve. You said this would be quick. Grab the girl and go." Carter was holding her wrists, trying to get her to stay still so he could cuff her to the bed. He managed to get one cuff secure. He wiped sweat from his brow with the back of his hand. He was worried. Good. Because he'd sealed his fate the second he'd stepped foot in this house with Steve.

"Shut up!" I watched in horror as Steve pulled a handgun from his waistband and pointed it at Carter. I didn't give a fuck if he took Carter out, but he was next to Brie and that was a problem. What if Steve missed?

"Hey, Steve." I needed his attention on me. "Look, man, I gotta drain the pipes. Think you could untie me so—" The butt of his gun hit me in the temple, cutting off my question. My head flew to the side, and Brie's scream pierced the air. I slowly turned my head back to him, spots dancing in my vision. "A simple no would have been fine, asshole."

I looked at Carter, whose eyes grew wide, and decided to change tactics.

"How'd he convince you to do this, Carter? Money?"

"M-my wife is sick. Cancer." His eyes darted back and forth between me and Steve as if trying to determine which of us posed the biggest threat.

"I get that." Sad thing was, I sort of did. If Brie were sick, I'd move heaven and earth for her. But this? This was a line even I couldn't cross. "How'd you manage to get him out of jail?" I nodded my head toward Steve.

"Shut up!" Spit flew from Steve's mouth. "I'll kill both of you if you don't shut the hell up."

My mind raced. Jackson likely didn't even know Steve was gone, let alone that one of his deputies had been aiding him in his little plan. Also, if the power was knocked out, the security feed wasn't working, which meant no help would be coming. The pain in my head made it difficult to think, but I had to try. I was our only way out of this mess.

"So, what's the plan, Steve? What happens now?" I forced my attention to the man who had caused so much destruction.

"I think it's time to show Brie what a real man looks like." Steve went back to the foot of the bed and started to unbutton his pants.

"Now wait a—" Steve raised the gun and put a bullet

between Carter's eyes before he could finish his sentence. Brie screamed as blood splattered all over the wall, the bed, *her*.

"Jesus Christ." I tried to stand, but it was futile. I wasn't going anywhere. "What the fuck was that for?"

"He was getting on my nerves." He shrugged, as if murdering someone was an everyday occurrence. His voice sounded calm, in control. "Besides, I don't like an audience. I'll suffer through you being here because, quite frankly, I'll get almost as much satisfaction from your reaction as I will from her pussy."

Brie kicked as much as her cuffed legs allowed. She had one wrist free, but he wasn't close enough for her to do anything to him with that hand. He just laughed at her as he freed himself and pumped his dick a few times.

"I swear to God, you're a dead man." I was seething. "Do you hear me? Fucking dead!"

"P-p-please don't." Brie's head thrashed from side to side as she begged. My eyes zeroed in on her free hand stretching over the edge of the mattress.

What is she doing?

"Ah, pretty, don't you remember? I like it when you beg." He crawled onto the bed, and as he slid up her legs, his hands gripped her thighs. So hard her skin paled around the tips.

"Fuck you," she spat. She continued to stretch, but he seemed oblivious to the movement.

"Now, princess," he swiped blood from the corner of his mouth. "Is that any way to talk to a real man?" At the use of the hated nickname, Brie's face paled.

"I'm warning you—"

"What?" Steve pointed the gun at me. "What is it you think you can do to me from there?"

"I will fucking end you." As soon as the words left my

mouth, gunfire rang out and pain bloomed in my chest. Regret for not being able to save Brie was the last emotion I recognized before I was sucked into the black.

32

BRIE

Steve's limp body slammed down onto me. I'd managed to grab my gun from under my mattress just in time to put a bullet in his head as he pulled the trigger on Griffin. *Griffin!* I swiveled my head to the chair, and the instant I saw him, I knew he was dead.

I battled back tears as I shoved Steve off of me. He started to roll off the bed, but I managed to stop him from toppling over. I needed the keys to the handcuffs. I cringed as I searched his pockets, hating that I had to touch him. *Got 'em.* I freed my other wrist and shook my hands to restore blood flow.

I shoved Steve the rest of the way off the bed and had a small sense of satisfaction at the sound of his body hitting the floor. I uncuffed my feet and swung them over the edge. As I stood up, I grabbed the gun, just in case. I had to shake my legs to get the feeling to return, and once I did, I took a few steps to the chair... to Griffin. I collapsed in front of it, my head in his lap, and finally, I let the tears fall.

"I'm so sorry," I sobbed. "Griffin, I'm sorry. It's all my fault."

My head snapped up as the floor creaked, and I pointed my gun at the noise.

"Whoa, it's just me." Aiden stood in the doorway, lowering his gun while raising a hand in surrender. "I was on my way home and heard gunshots."

My hand fell back down, and the tears continued. Aiden rushed forward and sank to his knees next to me.

"What the fuck happened?" He reached out to put pressure on Griffin's wound. He glanced at me and snapped, "Brie, what happened?"

"Steve came and… he killed him." Sobs wracked my body. Aiden was still talking, but his words weren't registering.

"Brie. Snap out of it. He's not dead." His hand grabbed mine and shoved my palm against Griffin's neck. "Feel that? Brie, it's a pulse."

Slowly, the beat of Griffin's pulse registered, and I swiped the tears from my face. I scrambled to my feet. "He's alive?"

"Yeah, Brie. He's alive." Aiden stood, but maintained pressure on the wound. "We've gotta get him to the hospital. There's no phone service anywhere because of the damn storm, so it looks like it's you and me, babe."

I searched the room for my phone and spotted it on the floor next to the bed. I grabbed it and tried to dial out, but no luck. Aiden was right. We were on our own.

"I need you to keep pressure on his wound while I carry him outside to the Jeep. Can you do that?" His matter-of-fact tone centered me.

I grabbed a folded towel from my dresser and pressed it to Griffin's chest. I had no idea if he would make it. He'd lost a lot of blood, and there was no color to his skin. He was pasty white and cool to the touch. But I'd be damned if I didn't do everything I could to help.

"Good. I'm going to lift him, and I need you to keep up

with me. We need to be quick." I nodded and kept pressure on the towel as Aiden grunted under Griffin's weight.

We got him to the Jeep but had to put him in the cargo hold, as he was too heavy to maneuver into the back seat. I sat back there with him, never easing up the pressure.

"Griffin, you hold on. Do you hear me? I need you to come home." I talked to him the entire trip to town. "I need you, asshole. You don't get to die on me."

We reached the hospital, and Aiden threw the Jeep into park at the ER entrance. He ran inside to grab a doctor and came back out with Emersyn, Doc's girlfriend.

"What happened?" She asked as she opened the cargo door. "I need a gurney!" She yelled back inside to whoever was listening.

"He was shot. Once in the chest." A man appeared with a gurney, and he and Aiden managed to get Griffin onto it.

"Brie, you need to be checked out, too." Aiden gripped my hand when I tried to follow Griffin.

"I need to be with him." I fought his hold, but he didn't let up.

"He's in good hands. Let's find you a doctor." He guided me toward the reception desk and rapped his knuckles on the blue granite. "Can we get a doctor here?"

"Aiden, I'm fine. Please, just let me go with him."

"Honey, when he wakes up, he's gonna be madder than hell if I don't have you checked out. So, cooperate. Please? My life could depend on it." He managed to get through to me with that. He always had been able to use his sense of humor to charm others into doing what he wanted.

"Fine. But the second I'm cleared…"

"I'll get you in to see him. Cross my heart." He drew an X over his chest before turning back to the empty reception desk. This time, he pounded his fists before shouting, "For the love of God, can we get a doctor out here?"

"Sir, what seems to be the problem?" Aiden and I whipped around at the voice. "Oh, Miss Coleman. What brings you here?" Dr. Shall squinted at me.

"There was a bit of an *incident*," Aiden started. "Brie needs to be examined."

"Of course." Dr. Shall turned to walk away and threw a glance over his shoulder. "Follow me, please."

I followed the doctor who had treated the worst injuries I'd ever had and fought the wave of panic that threatened. I was fine. Steve was dead. I'd killed him.

"Please, Miss Coleman, put on this gown, and I'll be right back." Dr. Shall handed me a paper gown and exited the room.

Aiden had followed us, and he stood in the doorway.

"You can go." I wasn't about to change in front of him.

"Not happening." He turned his back to me. "That's the best you're getting."

I stripped out of my blood-soaked clothes and tossed them to the linoleum. I put the gown on and hopped onto the table.

"You can turn around now," I mumbled just as a knock sounded on the door. "Come in," I called.

Dr. Shall entered the room with Emersyn. I jumped off the table.

"How is he?" I demanded of her.

"He's in surgery. That's all I know." She shrugged, but sadness filtered into her eyes.

"What aren't you telling me?"

"Brie, let them check you over, then you can start interrogating." Aiden stepped next to me and guided me back up on the table.

"Fine, but if he dies on that table and I don't get to tell him—" My mouth snapped shut. Griffin should be the first person to hear those words from me.

"Babe, when he's out of surgery, you can tell him you love him a thousand times, okay?" Aiden crouched in front of me and stared into my eyes.

I nodded as a tear slid down my cheek.

33

GRIFFIN

"Brie, don't you think you should go home and get some rest?"

"I'll go home when he does, Aiden. Not a second before. Got it?"

I recognized the voices surrounding me and tried to find their source. Lead weights kept my eyes from opening.

"Aiden, did you see that? I think he's waking up." A small hand lifted my larger one. "Griff? Open your eyes for me."

I tried, but nothing happened.

"Nurse!" Aiden's voice carried, and I winced because it sounded like he was yelling into a microphone. A flurry of footsteps sounded in the room. "Brie saw his eyes move. Could he be waking up?"

"Griff? Come on, love. The doctor says the sooner you open your eyes, the sooner you can go home."

There was pressure on my arm, like someone was squeezing it. My finger twitched, and the pressure increased.

"Hey, Dr. Shall. Did you see that? His finger moved."

Blinding light pierced my eyes as my lids were lifted. The light wiggled back and forth, and a groan tore out of me.

"Mr. Strong. Can you hear me?" A cold hand picked mine up off the bed. "If you can hear me, squeeze my hand."

I gripped the hand with all my might.

"Good. That's good. A little weak, but we can work on that."

A little weak? That was not fucking weak.

"Mr. Strong, squeeze my hand if you feel this?" A tingling sensation trailed up the arch of my foot.

"Good. Now, can you open your eyes?"

The lead weight holding my lids closed slowly started to lift away. I managed to open them a little before slamming them shut again. My head throbbed, and the added stimulation didn't help.

"Griffin, you can do this." My hand was in a vice. "I know you can. It's been days since I saw your eyes. I need to see your eyes."

This time, I ignored the urge to slam my eyes shut again. As they adjusted to the light, I slowly swiveled my head from side to side, taking in four pairs of eyes staring at me.

"Welcome back, Mr. Strong." The doctor stepped closer to the bed while also looking at the machines I was hooked up to. "Everything looks good. Vitals are stable."

"What happened?" My voice was gritty from not being used.

"You were shot, Mr. Strong. Do you remember being shot?" Dr. Shall grabbed a chart from the hook on the wall and flipped through its pages. I remembered gunshots and pain, so I nodded. "The bullet pierced your chest and ricocheted off of a rib before it tore through your spleen. We had to remove your spleen, and while we were there, we managed to get all of the bullet fragments out. You also had a nasty contusion to the back of your head, so we've had you in a medically induced coma to reduce swelling on the brain."

"How long?"

"Four days, man." Aiden spoke from the foot of the bed. "We were starting to worry." He pointed to the woman to my right and laughed.

My head fell to the side, and I took in the sight next to me. Brie's eyes were bright with unshed tears, and she gave me a wobbly smile.

"I'm sorry," I croaked. Her tears fell. "Don't cry. I can't stand it."

"I'm just happy you're okay." She lifted my hand to her lips and pressed a kiss to my palm. As she laid my hand back down, she blew out a ragged breath. "I need some coffee." She stood, and that's when I noticed the blue hospital scrubs she was wearing. When she reached the door, she paused and glanced over her shoulder. "I'll be right back." With that, she was gone.

Lines of worry creased my forehead and Aiden must have seen it.

"I'll go with her. Make sure she's okay." He took off after her.

"Honey, I'm going to help you sit up and see if you can take small sips of water for me, okay?" A grandmotherly nurse filled the spot where Brie had been. I grunted and groaned as she helped me sit up, and when she finally had the damn pillows where she thought they should be, her gaze caught mine. "You've got a keeper there." She nodded toward the door where Brie had exited. "Never left your side. Put up one heck of a fight when she was told only family could stay. Said she was your family, and if anyone claimed otherwise, well, she'd shove a boot up their…" She cleared her throat. "Well, you know." Her voice had lowered to a whisper, like she was telling me a dirty secret.

"That's my girl." A smile bloomed on my face at the thought of Brie going toe to toe with hospital personnel. A pink plastic cup of water was brought to my lips, and I sucked in the cold liquid through the straw, letting it glide down my throat to ease the hoarseness.

"Mr. Strong, if all goes well, you'll be out of here in a few days." Dr. Shall replaced the chart on the hook. "Do you have any questions for me?"

"Is Brie okay? How bad was she hurt?"

"I'm sorry, Mr. Strong, but I can't discuss—"

"Honey, she's going to be just fine. Don't you worry none." The nurse cut him off. He gave her a look that said they'd be talking about this later, but he didn't speak. She rolled her eyes at his expression and refocused her attention on me. "Now, do you need anything before we leave?"

"No, ma'am."

"Okay then. You just rest, and when Miss Brie comes back, I'll send her in."

"Thank you." I turned my head toward Dr. Shall. "And thank you, doc."

"No thanks necessary. I'll be back in a few hours to check on you."

Left to my own devices, my mind wound back over what had gone down at Brie's cabin. When I'd come to and seen Brie on the bed with those two maniacs holding her down, I experienced a sense of helplessness I never had before. She'd been right in front of me, and I couldn't save her. And then I'd been shot. I absently touched the spot on my chest that was covered in bandages. *Fuck.* I could only imagine what she'd endured after that.

"Get that look off your face." My head snapped to where Brie stood leaning against the door frame, a steaming Styrofoam cup in her hands.

"What look?"

"That look," she pushed off the frame and walked toward me, "that says 'I failed her.'" She dropped in the chair next to the bed and set her cup down on the bedside table. She leaned her elbows on the bed and lifted my hand. "You did not fail me."

"Baby, I'm so sorry I didn't do more."

"Would you stop? Look at me. I'm fine." She leaned back so I could get a good look. "See, fine."

"What happened after I was shot?" I was terrified of the answer, but I couldn't quite bring myself to believe that she hadn't suffered more. She had to have injuries that I couldn't see.

"I freaked out." She averted her eyes. "I thought you were dead and—"

"What about Steve?"

"I killed him." Her eyes bore into mine, daring me to question her further. I didn't. "Anyway, I managed to get the key and free myself and…" She shook her head and squeezed her eyes shut.

"Look at me."

Her eyes slowly opened, and a few tears slid down her cheek before she wiped them away.

"Baby, I'm right here." I picked her hand up and held it tightly between my own. "You're not getting rid of me that easily."

"Griffin, I…" Her irises blazed and locked onto mine.

"What, baby?"

"When I thought you were dead, it was like, I don't know, my world shattered into a million little pieces. And I had no idea how to put them back together again. Not without you. No matter what, you were always there to make me whole. And the thought of never being able to tell you that I love you or not having the opportunity to ride through this life with you…" She shook her head. "I wanted to die too."

"You love me?"

"So goddamn much."

EPILOGUE

BRIE

One year later...

"Are you ready for this?" Sadie stood to my right as we stared at our reflections in the mirror.

"So ready." I grabbed her hand and squeezed.

"You both look stunning. I can't wait to see their faces when you walk down the aisle." Nell chuckled. "They're so screwed."

"Well, shall we?" I cocked my elbow and Sadie locked arms with me.

"Let's do this."

As we walked through the main house toward the back yard where we would marry our best friends, I couldn't help but think about how far we'd all come.

When Griffin had gotten out of the hospital, he'd officially moved in with me. His cabin hadn't sat empty for long. Doc had moved in with his girlfriend, Emersyn, and they were recently engaged.

Griffin and I continued to take things one day at a time, but I stopped holding back. When I told him I loved him, I meant it, and not a day went by that I didn't tell him that. Life was uncertain, and I never wanted him to doubt how I felt.

There had been an investigation into Steve and Carter, even though both were dead. Jackson took the deception of one of his deputies pretty hard, but Griffin had set him straight. It hadn't been Jackson's fault any more than it had been mine or Griff's. No one blamed Jackson but Jackson.

When we reached the arch covered in white lilies, we paused and waited for the music to start. The first few notes of Ed Sheeran's "Thinking Out Loud" played, and Sadie and I walked, arms linked, toward our men. Our sweet, overbearing, protective, *hot* men.

Griffin's eyes never wavered from mine. When we reached them, Sadie and I separated and stood next to our respective grooms.

"You look beautiful." Griffin leaned in and grazed my cheek with his lips. "Absolutely fuckable." His breath teased my ear before he stood straight.

Heat rose up my neck and spread across my cheeks. I prayed that no one had heard him, but Aiden's snort told me my prayer had been wasted.

"If we may begin," the preacher said in an admonishing tone.

"Of course." Micah glared at Griffin, but the corners of his mouth tilted upward.

"Dearly beloved, we are gathered here today to join these men and these women in holy matrimony." I didn't hear another word until it was time to say our vows. Micah and Sadie went first, and by the time they were done, I was struggling to hold on to my composure.

When it was our turn, I faced Griffin and we held hands.

"Brie, you have been the driving force behind my existence for so long. When I first laid eyes on you, you took my breath away. Over the years, you have only gotten more beautiful, inside and out. Not a day goes by that I don't thank my lucky stars for you, and I will spend every day for the rest of my life cherishing you. I love you more than any stuff."

My chin wobbled at his use of the phrase we said every night to each other. I took a deep breath and started my vows.

"Griffin, you are my light when I'm surrounded by the dark. You are my breath when I feel I have no air left. You have shown me in a thousand different ways what love is, and I am so grateful that you never gave up on me. I will spend every day for the rest of my life being not only your wife, but doing everything I can to be worthy of the title. I love you more than any stuff."

The rest of the ceremony passed in a blur until the preacher pronounced us husband and wife. I didn't even wait until he said the words 'You may kiss the bride' before throwing my arms around Griffin's neck, and my lips crashed with his. He chuckled into my mouth before diving into the kiss, his tongue sweeping across my lips and past their seam.

"Hi, Mrs. Strong," Griffin whispered when he pulled back.

"Hi." My lips stretched to reach his for a quick peck.

"Congrats." Aiden slapped Griffin on the back and gave me a quick hug. "Now, let's go party."

"God help us all." Micah laugh behind us.

~

Griffin

As I danced with my wife, I couldn't help but think back over all the times I'd dreamt of this moment. She was the only woman I'd ever loved and despite all the odds that had been against us, we were here. Married.

"I love you." She looked up at me with bright eyes. Eyes that I'd worried I'd never see the light in again.

"I love you too." I spun her around and dipped her, loving the view of her back arched and her breasts peeking out of her dress. "We need to get out of here. Soon," I growled into her ear when I pulled her back up.

"We haven't even had cake yet." She poked her bottom lip out, something I'd learned I had no defenses against.

"Fine. Let's go cut the cake." I stopped dancing and tugged her by the hand toward the twin cakes on the round table in the corner, not stopping until we reached it.

"So impatient. Is this what life with you is going to be like?" Her hand graced the hip that she had cocked out.

"Like what? Me being impatient to fuck you anytime I lay eyes on you?" I shrugged. "Probably. But you can handle it." I winked at her and she blushed.

We spent the next five minutes bickering about cake and sex.

"Aww, you guys having your first fight?" Aiden threw an arm around both of us. "Tell papa Aiden all about it."

"Fuck off." I elbowed him in the gut.

He clutched his side, pretending it hurt. After a few more minutes of razzing each other, Aiden pulled his phone out of his pocket. "I want to get a picture of—" His eyes widened when he looked at the screen.

"What is it?" Brie put her arm on his and leaned over to look at his phone. "Who's Scarlett?"

"Uh, no one. Sorry, guys, but I've gotta go." Aiden didn't bother looking up from the screen as he walked off.

"What was that about?" Brie looked at me with questions in her eyes.

"No idea." I scooped her up in my arms, and she squealed.

"Griffin, don't you want to know what's going on?" Her head pillowed on my shoulder as her arms came around my neck.

"Nope. All I want to do right now is take my wife home, strip her naked and fuck her senseless." My cock was growing painfully hard just thinking about it.

"Well then. What kind of wife would I be to deny her husband?" She kissed me as I carried her past all of the wedding guests up to the main house.

When we got to the steps of the porch, she pulled away and framed my face in her hands and shook her head.

"What, baby?"

Fire sparked in her eyes before she leaned her forehead on mine and said one of the things I'd never tire of hearing.

"Take me home, Griffin."

BONUS CHAPTER

Need more of Griffin and Brie? Sign up for my newsletter at andirhodes.com for an EXCLUSIVE bonus chapter, as well as updates on upcoming novels and giveaways.

SNEAK PEEK AT BROKEN BOUNDARIES

BOOK THREE IN THE BROKEN REBEL BROTHERHOOD SERIES

Aiden...

I hate secrets. They ruin people's lives and end relationships. Too bad I picked a job that's full of clients with skeletons in their closet. None of that bothers me because I can compartmentalize. Keep the required boundaries in tact. Until she shows up on my doorstep.

She's the one person that can make me forget the rules of the brotherhood. The only person I would even consider doing that for. Problem is, she has one secret that's a game changer. And it's one I'm not sure I can forgive.

Scarlett...

I can take care of myself. Or so I thought. I never expected to need his protection again, but that doesn't change the facts. I do need him, more than I ever have before. But when he finds out my secret, will he still be willing to protect me?

I fell in love with him the first time I met him, and despite walking away and staying gone for four years, my feelings haven't changed. Nor has the explosive chemistry between us. I'm just not sure he feels the same or if I'm just another client.

PROLOGUE

AIDEN

*F*ucking weddings.

I hated them, but I was the best man so I had to be here. At least Micah and Griffin hadn't made me wear a monkey suit. That would have been pure torture. Griffin was currently arguing with his wife, Brie, and I was enjoying the show. Married a little over an hour and they were already fighting.

I sauntered over to the cake table to join them. "Aww, you guys having your first fight?" I slung my arms around their shoulders. "Tell papa Aiden all about it."

"Fuck off." Griffin elbowed me in the gut.

"Damn, man." I clutched my side, feigning hurt. Had Griffin put his full strength behind it, there would have been no pretending on my part. Brie was laughing at us, and I glared at her. "What's so funny?"

"You two. You're ridiculous." Her laughter continued for a few minutes, and I didn't have the heart to give her a hard time about it. She'd been through a lot recently, and it was great to see her happy.

Wanting to capture the moment, I pulled my phone out of

my pocket. "I want to get a picture of—" My eyes widened when I looked at the screen. "Fuck," I muttered.

"What is it?" Brie put her arm on mine and leaned over to look at the phone. "Who's Scarlett?"

"Uh, no one. Sorry, guys, but I've gotta go." I didn't bother looking up from the screen as I walked off and headed toward my bike.

When I reached Calypso, my Harley Davidson Street Bob, I straddled her and glanced at the text I'd received.

Scarlett: I hope u remember me. Need ur help. Meet me at Dusty's.

Did I remember her? Of course I fucking remembered her. I didn't bother taking the time to text her back before I pulled out of the driveway and pointed Calypso toward the little dive bar the brotherhood liked to frequent.

As I drove the country roads, I thought back to the day Scarlett had showed up asking for the help and protection of the Broken Rebel Brotherhood. She'd been twenty-three and drop-dead gorgeous. That had been two years ago, and at the time, she claimed to have a stalker. From the moment I answered the door to see her standing on the other side, I'd made mistake after mistake.

Rather than scheduling an appointment with her, like we always did with potential clients, I'd taken one look at her terrified demeanor and offered her a place to stay on BRB property, no questions asked. More precisely, I'd offered her a room in my own cabin.

Mistake number one.

At first, I'd stayed at the main house to give Scarlett privacy. Unfortunately, I found myself making up excuses to go see her. Sure, some of it had been legit. I'd needed to check on her, make sure she didn't need anything. I'd also had to get changes of clothes when I'd dirtied all I had at the main house.

Mistake number two.

Before I knew it, excuses were no longer necessary and I was back to staying at my own house, in my own bed... and she'd been in it with me.

Mistake number three.

I pulled into the parking lot at Dusty's and barely got the bike parked before hopping off and striding into the dimly lit bar.

"Yo, Aiden. Aren't you supposed to be at the wedding?" Dusty paused what he was doing and raised a hand in greeting.

"I was." I scanned the bar and noted there were fewer patrons than normal. *Probably all back at the reception.* My gaze landed back on Dusty's face. "Was there a woman in here? Blonde and about yea tall." I held my hand up in front of my chest to indicate Scarlett's height.

Dusty's eyes narrowed in thought. "Nope. Not that I recall." He swiveled around to yell back to the kitchen. "Hey, Kara! You see a blonde-haired chick in here at all tonight?"

Kara came through the swinging partition and gave me a cheeky grin. "Hey, Aiden."

She was beautiful, and at one time we'd had sex, but I had zero interest in a repeat performance. Not that she wasn't a nice woman, but there was only one female that I was interested in sharing a bed with longterm and she'd taken off two years ago. "Can't say that I've seen any women here tonight. Everyone's at the wedding." Her hand was on her cocked hip as she spoke. "Who is she?"

Disappointment flooded my system. I rubbed the back of my neck and ignored Kara's question. Before sitting on a stool, I pulled my phone out of my pocket. "You sure? Name's Scarlett." I opened a photo I had saved and turned the phone for them to look at it. "This is an older picture, but I imagine she looks about the same." I hoped she looked the same.

Both shook their heads.

"Sorry, man," Dusty said. "Hey, you want a drink while you're here?" He bent to grab a glass from under the bar. "On the house."

"Yeah, sure." What I *really* wanted was to punch something. "Whatever is fine." I heaved a sigh and stared at Scarlett's photo. It had been taken one morning after breakfast. She was standing in front of the sink, rinsing dishes, and I'd made some smart ass comment to get her to turn around. Her lips were slightly parted, and there were creases at the corners of her eyes because she'd laughed at whatever I'd said. My dick got hard, and I shifted on the stool.

Fuck this.

Me: Where r u? I'm at the bar.

I silently berated myself for texting her as I set the phone on the bar-top, screen down, and took a gulp of the ice-cold beer Dusty had sat in front of me. As the cool liquid settled in my gut, my phone pinged with an incoming text. I didn't immediately look at it. Instead, I ordered a shot of Fireball. As the whiskey burned a path down my throat, I felt a little more fortified and picked up my phone.

Scarlett: Sorry

Seriously? That's all she had to say? I raised two fingers in the air, indicating to Dusty that I wanted two more shots. When they were placed in front of me, I made short work of downing them both.

"You gonna need a ride home tonight, man?" Dusty's brows dipped in concern.

"Probably." I rarely drank to the point of oblivion, but I planned on it tonight. "Just don't call Micah or Griffin."

"Got it." He chuckled as he picked up the cordless phone to place a call. "Wouldn't want to interrupt the wedding night." He cackled, actually cackled, like an old gossipy woman. "Hey, Doc," he said into the phone. "Aiden's gonna need a ride tonight. Come get him in an hour or two?" I didn't hear the other side of the conversation, but I assumed Doc agreed.

And if he didn't? Fuck it. I'd be too drunk to give a damn where I slept, and the bar floor was as good a place as any.

ABOUT THE AUTHOR

Andi Rhodes is an author whose passion is creating romance from chaos in all her books! She writes MC (motorcycle club) romance with a generous helping of suspense and doesn't shy away from the more difficult topics. Her books can be triggering for some so consider yourself warned. Andi also ensures each book ends with the couple getting their HEA! Most importantly, Andi is living her real life HEA with her husband and their boxers.

For access to release info, updates, and exclusive content, be sure to sign up for Andi's newsletter at andirhodes.com.

ALSO BY ANDI RHODES

Broken Rebel Brotherhood

Broken Souls

Broken Innocence

Broken Boundaries

Broken Rebel Brotherhood: Complete Series Box set

Broken Rebel Brotherhood: Next Generation

Broken Hearts

Broken Wings

Broken Mind

Bastards and Badges

Stark Revenge

Slade's Fall

Jett's Guard

Soulless Kings MC

Fender

Joker

Piston

Greaser

Riker

Trainwreck

Squirrel

Gibson

Satan's Legacy MC

Snow's Angel

Toga's Demons

Magic's Torment

Printed in Great Britain
by Amazon